To a wonderful friend, Anne, from Emily

The Pembroke Path

by

Emily Cary

Copyright 2012 Emily Cary All Rights Reserved.

Table of Contents

1.	Invitation to a Murder	1
2.	Evading the Stalker	12
3.	Green Room Guests	21
4.	Television Talk Show	32
5.	The Bold Proposition	43
6.	Journey to Pembrokeshire	53
7.	The First Victim	67
8.	Probing the Unknown	79
9.	Nevern and the Holy Rood	93
10.	Ghosts of Antiquity	106
11.	Welsh Voices	119
12.	Torquaytoons Unmasked	130
13.	Mystical Welsh Traditions	143
14.	Holy Grail Connection	159
15.	The Abduction	172
16.	The Twelfth Victim	189
17.	Invitation to the Future	199

CHAPTER ONE

Invitation to a Murder

I was still an ingénue in the theater of pseudonyms when the conductor entered the First Class coach and examined my BritRail Pass. "First time here, Luv?"

"Basically, yes," I said. "My parents brought me to London when I was small, but it's all a blur."

"Well, you're almost home."

I must have looked puzzled because he chuckled and tapped my signature on the pass with his forefinger. "Your name, Luv. It's as Welsh as Merlin the magician."

My true identity bared, I returned his grin. "You've pegged me. Once I've taken care of some business in Bristol, I plan to spend a few days in Wales for some research."

"To get in touch with your heritage, is it?"

"That, too." He moved on down the aisle before I could add that my primary goal was to investigate a mystery.

The man seated across from me had been absorbed in *The London Times,* but as I returned the rail pass to my purse, I sensed that he had assessed the brief exchange. Like the other conservatively dressed businessmen seated in our coach, he exuded typical British reserve, discreetly focusing his gaze on the newspaper. Following suit, I concentrated on the task at hand.

Ever since the train left Paddington Station, I had been reviewing my notes, choosing meaty points I hoped would interest the television audience. Like most American writers, I was humbled by the ever-present aura of my British counterparts descended from the world's greatest literary tradition. Starkly aware that my sole attempt at investigative journalism paled in comparison, I felt even more inadequate the closer the high-speed train drew to Bristol.

Unaccustomed to speaking before an audience, especially one the size of that reached by ITV, Britain's independent network, I dared not dwell on the fact that millions of viewers might be tuned in. It was scant consolation to know that I would be merely one member of a talk-show panel in a studio far less formidable than London's BBC; the butterflies in my stomach were beginning to multiply.

And no wonder. During my stint as a journalist, I functioned in a solitary world devoid of wearisome staff meetings and office banter. My beat was limited to gathering court records and entering them into the newspaper office computer, sometimes in person, more often by modem from my laptop computer. When time allowed, I leafed through early documents for records of unsolved crimes, never dreaming that I would happen upon papers destined to detour my career from local newspaper reporter to hardcover best seller with the added bonanza of royalty checks. I still gasp each time I enter a book store and see a prominent display of my very own book: *The Rittenhouse Murder* by Tara Tyler.

That's not my real name. Roberta Whitney, my editor at Olsen Books, dreamed it up to spare me the wrath of a prominent Philadelphia family, a strong possibility, because my investigation of a turn-of-the-century murder uncovered evidence to implicate the husband of the society matron victim. The elusive intruder he convinced the police was to blame never existed. Four generations later, his descendants might take exception to my findings, despite irrefutable proof. My out, Bertie concluded, was to craft a roman à clef to tap the vast audience of mystery fans.

Having shopped my manuscript around for two years without an agent to intercede on my behalf, I cherished my good fortune and was not about to argue with Bertie, who plucked it from the slush pile and gave it wheels. If she had asked me to refashion it as a household plumbing maintenance manual, I would have complied cheerfully. At that juncture, nothing mattered except holding the published fruits of my research in my hands, even if the name on the front of the book jacket was foreign to the face on the back, one known to friends and family as Sarah Morgan.

Sarah the reporter could not have afforded a seat in the First Class compartment of the Great Western express train, but Tara the novelist was taking advantage of her publisher's largesse. Now that Tara Tyler was becoming a known quantity in the mystery genre, it was time to increase her output and I believed that a trip to

Wales would provide the raw material for her second best seller.

Even before the book tour materialized, I became intrigued by newspaper accounts of young women vanishing, one by one, while walking on the Pembroke Path, a popular hiking trail alongside the Irish seacoast. Now I would take advantage of this unexpected opportunity to scour the area and investigate their lifestyles for clues to their fate. Should nothing substantial surface, I felt certain that my imagination would devise a solution to the mystery, along with the obligatory love story. Elated by my proposal, Bertie rang Olsen's London branch to request they grant me ample time during my publicity tour to research my next mystery novel.

Six hours after Bertie saw me off from the Philadelphia airport, I staggered through Heathrow customs, battling jet lag and scanning the waiting crowd for her counterpart, Elspeth Wentworth, who had arranged to meet me there. It did not help that London time was nine in the morning, while my internal clock was slogging through the wee hours back home in Pennsylvania.

"Yoo hoo, Sarah, Tara. Elspeth here."

The woman hailing me as I emerged from the security passageway towered over many of the men also awaiting arriving passengers. With the vigor of a field hockey fullback, she muscled forward to grab my arm with one hand, my suitcase with the other, and shouldered our path directly through the throng to the queue of London's famous black cabs waiting at the entrance.

Elspeth was detail personified. The moment I sank into the taxi's roomy seat, she began directing the cabbie through each twist and turn that she assured him would shorten the distance to the flat she had rented for me in Mayfair. Tall and lanky, and blessed with the dewy English complexion that shuns makeup, Elspeth spoke in the brisk, confidential manner of one who assumes that the listener comprehends every word uttered. Whether the fault lay with my jet lag or her tweedy Oxford accent that muffled key syllables, I had trouble participating in the conversation, except when she paused to chortle heartily about a remark she had just made. I hoped my weak laughter was sufficient response to assure her my head was on straight.

By the time we reached the flat, I had accumulated a sheaf of directions to the interviews, readings, and book signings she had arranged. Elspeth explained that they were scattered throughout the month to allow me ample time to travel about on my own and gather data for my next book, as Bertie had requested. Judiciously, she saved my London appearances at the BBC studio, Hatchard's, Waterman's, and other city booksellers for the final week. By that time, she assured me, I would feel more comfortable speaking before audiences of British mystery fans who cut their eye teeth on Sir Conan Doyle and Agatha Christie.

"They'll take to you as soon as they turn the first page of your book," she promised. "You're a born storyteller."

Initially, Elspeth had been convincing, but now that I was headed for my British television debut, I felt queasy. Had I not been so worried, I might have relaxed, swept my laptop from the table between us to allow the passenger facing me more room for his newspaper, and leaned back to admire the lush Thames Valley rushing past the window. Backward seating made the pastoral scenes retreating at high speed play tricks on my eyes, so I focused on my notes, trying to devise brief, illuminating remarks in response to generic questions the moderator might pose. I did not look up until the woman propelling the refreshment cart through the coach paused to offer a beverage.

I dug into my purse for my wallet. "Coffee, please."

"It's complimentary in First Class, Luv," she said, as she poured a steaming cup from the silver pitcher on her cart. "Care for a biscuit?"

"Biscuit?"

In response, she tossed a cellophane packet of oatmeal cookies onto the table, reminding me that not all English words mean the same on both sides of the Atlantic. "I'll have a bottle of still water," the man opposite said. "No biscuits."

"Here you are, sir." The attendant placed the bottle of water, a plastic cup, and a napkin before him, then shoved the refreshment cart past us to the next passengers.

The man set aside his newspaper, uncapped the bottle, and was about to fill his cup when the unmistakable ring of a mobile phone diverted his attention. As he drew the instrument from his breast pocket, I peered at my computer screen, pretending to ignore his conversation. That was impossible.

"Trevor here." He spoke in a hushed, intense voice. "Right...Thanks for ringing me up...No, you're not mistaken...That's exactly what I meant. We have to get rid of her right away...Use your imagination...It can look like an accident...How should I know? You're the creative genius...Of course, I'll contribute what I can, but I leave it to you to devise an ingenious way to finish her off. Something that won't look contrived...A car accident's always an easy out. Maybe the accelerator sticks and she sails off a pier. Just be sure the water's deep enough to keep her submerged...An airplane? I don't think so. That would involve others...Sky-diving? Hmmm, that's different. We could move things along quickly without leaving any frayed ends."

I dared not look at the man. Trevor, he called himself. My heart pounded, my palms glistened with sweat as the gist of his conversation hit home. Fate had seated me inches away from a murderer, one devoid of scruples. He was so evil and sure of himself that he had no fear an American overhearing him would alert the authorities. Well, he had another think coming. My ploy was to play it cool until I reached Bristol. There I would march directly to the railroad security office and convince them to detain him for as long as necessary. He was not going to kill a hapless woman if I had any say in the matter. For all I knew, he could be the villain behind the Pembrokeshire crimes.

He continued speaking to the caller in a smooth, untroubled manner, a cold-hearted criminal if I ever heard one. "Where am I now?" – this in response to a question on the other end. "The white horse is just ahead, so we're about halfway to Bristol. I'll be there for the better part of the day, and then I'll head on out to Pembrokeshire. I'll call you from there."

Pembrokeshire! I choked on the oatmeal biscuit. By accident, I had stumbled upon the man the authorities had not yet apprehended. I was still coughing when I realized he had switched off his phone and was speaking to me.

"Would you care for a sip of my water?"

"Your...water?" I stared at him and coughed again.

"Yes, it might help. You're having trouble swallowing that biscuit. They're tasty, but terribly dry. That's why I don't take them when offered."

"No thank you. I'm quite all right."

He shrugged. "As you wish. I'm happy to share."

"I hardly think so." There was unmistakable finality in my tone. This vicious man deserved no thanks from me. To avoid his stare, I turned my gaze toward the window, and there beheld what he had viewed from his vantage point. A great white horse carved from chalkstone monopolized the distant green hillock, a truly remarkable work of art from the past. My eyes followed it until the train rounded the next bend and the horse slipped from sight. Surely the primitive men who created it could not imagine the evil that was passing before it several millenniums later.

At the very moment I was calculating my next move, deciding how to elude the murderer at the Bristol station, my own phone rang. "Yes?" I spoke tentatively, not wishing to divulge any information that would give Trevor reason to suspect my plans.

The voice at the other end was uncommonly cheerful. "Tara, it's Elspeth. I hope you had a pleasant evening and a chance to rest."

"Yes, thank you. The flat is lovely."

"Where are you now?"

"We've just passed a white horse."

"Good, good." Elspeth's merry laughter brightened my precarious situation. "If you're that far along, you must have made the earlier train. That means there's plenty of time. You don't have to report to the studio until three, so I suggest you take a break and alight at Bath. The Pump Room and Roman Baths are well worth a look and you should have ample time to take them in before heading on to Bristol. They're only two blocks from the station, and the trains run every half hour."

"But…the last leg…how long?" I let the question dangle, not wishing to ask aloud the length of the ride from Bath to Bristol.

"Ten, fifteen minutes at the most. They're only a few miles apart."

Slowly, I said, "That just might work." This unexpected diversion would give me a chance to contact the authorities at Bath, earlier than I had anticipated. Trevor could be picked up the moment this train pulled into Bristol.

"So glad I caught you," Elspeth said. "It wouldn't do for you to miss one of Jane Austen's favorite cities. Writers tend to have similar tastes."

"Your call came at the perfect moment."

"How so?"

"I'll explain when I see you. Bye."

I launched my exit plot by closing the laptop and returning it to my overnight bag, then looped the purse handle over my arm. Trevor had overheard my conversation with the conductor and knew that Bristol was my original destination. To avoid suspicion, I would wait until the train was stopped at Bath and the doors were ajar before bolting from my seat.

Things did not transpire exactly as I hoped. When the train pulled into Bath, I waited for the conductor to announce our arrival. That never happened. Only when I glanced out the window and saw him on the station platform signaling the engine did I realize the train was about to depart. As I bounded into the aisle, the purse dragged across the table, knocking over Trevor's open water bottle and my half empty coffee cup.

"Blast!" He jumped to his feet to escape the liquid spreading across the table.

Under any other circumstances, I would have offered an apology and helped mop up the mess, but I was so distraught that the devil overcame me and I hissed, "Serves you right, you evil man."

"*What?*"

His eyes flashed with what I read as intent to strangle me. I fled to the exit and down the steps just as the train began to move. Several poky passengers on the platform caused a bottleneck, forcing me into a slow procession down the staircase to the street level. I was about to search for the station superintendent when a shout from behind chilled my blood.

"I say, young lady! Just one moment!"

I glanced over my shoulder. He was no more than

ten feet away waving his arm and scowling for all the world as if he had targeted me for execution. Apparently he took his victims wherever they materialized and I was his immediate choice.

CHAPTER TWO

Evading the Stalker

Terrified, I abandoned my mission to report him to the railway police in favor of finding refuge at the Roman Baths. I stumbled out of the train station onto the sidewalk, saw that the pedestrian lights were in my favor, and made a dash for it. Just in time. Once I was across the street, the lights changed and the idling cars gunned forward, giving me a head start on my pursuer.

Not daring to look behind, I concentrated on my options up ahead. For as far as I could see, camera-toting tourists confirmed that I was headed toward the town's main attractions. To widen the gulf between Trevor and me, I zigzagged through the crowd, clutching my overnight bag with one hand while the purse jiggled wildly on my arm. Once I had gone some distance and felt more confident about my progress, I glanced back. He was nowhere in sight. I took this as proof that he had given up and returned to the station for the next train to Bristol.

The throng of pedestrians ahead of me had traveled no more than the two blocks Elspeth had promised when they turned as one into a large square dominated by an imposing cathedral. Could the Pump

Room and Roman Baths be nearby?

An elderly woman, noticing my hesitation, caught my arm. "If you're looking for the Pump Room, it's right through there." She pointed to a low building of Georgian design directly across the square.

"How did you know...?"

She smiled. "Everyone goes to the Pump Room. If you want to see the Roman Baths, the ticket counter and entryway are inside."

Thanking her, I hurried toward the Pump Room, its unobtrusive sign blocked by a sea of visitors. Slipping into line, I moved with the flow into an elegant hall where a string quartet serenaded diners seated at beautifully appointed tables. On the far side of the room, a queue of tourists had formed to sample the curative powers of water pumped by a young man attired in the garb of an 18th Century servant.

The serene atmosphere was exactly what my rattled nerves needed, so I queued up at the reservation desk where the maître d' and an assistant were taking the names of those wishing to be accommodated. Ten minutes later, few had been dispatched to tables, no doubt because many of those seated chose to linger in the luxurious setting. I was about to consult my watch when someone clutched my wrist. For one chilling moment, I feared that Trevor had found me, but the sight of perfectly manicured nails sporting a vivid magenta polish eased the terror rising in my throat.

"I'm sorry to trouble you," the woman began, "but my daughter and I would like a table for two and we're told that there will be a long wait. However, they have plenty of larger tables available, and since you seem to be alone, I wonder if you'd mind sharing one with us. That way, we both can be served sooner."

"Why, thank you. That's very kind. I have an engagement in Bristol and was just beginning to worry that there won't be time to eat and see the Roman Baths before I have to leave."

She beamed. "Wonderful. Come to the head of the line with me and I'll change our reservation to a party of three."

That did the trick. We were soon seated, I with an unbroken view of the musicians on stage, my companions facing the costumed Pumper dispensing glasses of spa water. Before we had time to consult the menu, our waitress recited such intriguing daily specials that we opted for several of her suggestions in place of the standard dishes. She whisked away to the kitchen, leaving us to introduce ourselves.

Betty Ambler and her daughter Dawn, I quickly learned, were fellow Americans, each with a separate agenda. "I brought Dawn over to get a bit of culture," Betty said. "I thought a trip to Great Britain would be a nice influence after all the tackiness she's exposed to in the States."

Dawn did not share either her mother's enthusiasm or sense of style. Next to Betty's classic suit, Dawn looked like a refugee from a brothel. I reminded myself that her attire was no worse than that of any typical American teenager one might see strolling through a New Jersey mall in spaghetti straps and low-rise jeans. It was a bit much, however, in England and particularly in Bath, where elegant society once convened. Dawn spoke when prompted, but seem sullen and visibly resentful of her mother's attempt to wean her from the ways of her peers.

"I'm sure you'll have a wonderful time, Dawn," I said, trying to be encouraging. "This is my first trip, too, and I'm going to take advantage of every minute and see as many famous sights as I can stuff into each day. You'll have ever so much to talk about with your friends back home."

Dawn rolled her eyes and muttered, "I suppose so."

Betty smiled at her, the sad smile often seen on mothers not wishing to upset their teenagers, but convinced, nevertheless, that some improvement is in order. We chatted briefly about their itinerary until several women leaving an adjacent table paused by my chair. "We can't take our eyes off you," one gushed. "You look so familiar. My friend thinks you're that writer…what's-her-name?"

"Tyler. Tara Tyler," the other prompted.

"Well, actually that's who I am," I admitted.

"Tara Tyler?" Betty nearly jumped from her chair. "But you told us your name is Sarah Morgan."

"I'm not trying to confuse you. I really am Sarah, but my editor saddled me with a pseudonym that's becoming more trouble than it's worth."

Betty was ecstatic. "Hear that, Dawn? We're having lunch with a celebrity."

For the first time in my presence, Dawn smiled. "Do you know any other celebrities?"

"Sorry to disappoint you, but I'm not a celebrity

and I've never met one. Maybe that will change while I'm in England because my editor has arranged for me to be on a couple of talk shows, but I assure you I'll be just as awestruck by the hosts and guests as you would be."

"Talk shows, wow!" Dawn was visibly impressed.

Nothing I said subdued the ladies lingering at our table. They effervesced until our meal arrived, prodding me to sign the envelopes and business cards they extracted from the depths of their purses for themselves and friends back home.

By the time our house salad and yeasty bread direct from the oven were followed by a cheddar quiche, my presence had attracted additional attention from the staff and surrounding diners. Sensing eyes upon me from all sides of the room, I paid extra attention to my table manners and hoped I could refrain from making a *faux pas*. Now I knew the downside of celebrity, if that is what I was experiencing.

The meal over, we agreed to view the wonders of the Roman Baths together after a quick stop in the ladies' room. Betty and I were reapplying our lipstick when Dawn, who had been waiting in the hallway, came bursting in.

"The cutest guy asked about you," she said.

I stiffened. "Guy? What guy?"

"He didn't give his name, but he wanted to know yours because he noticed you at our table and thought you looked like an old friend. I saw him drinking a glass of water at the pump and staring at you while we ate."

I blanched white. "What did he look like?"

"He was hot."

"Dawn, how many times have I told you that's not a ladylike expression." Betty looked at me in despair and shook her head. "The terms they pick up from television and films would have grounded me when I was her age."

I grabbed Dawn's arm. "Was he wearing a dark suit?"

"I don't remember. I didn't pay attention to his suit, but he was really cute."

"Where is he now?"

"He's gone. After I told him both of your names, he thanked me and left."

I exhaled. "Just like that? You're sure he's not waiting around?"

"Is there a problem?" Betty looked concerned. "Not a stalker, I hope."

Worse than that, I thought. I tried to smile. "I doubt it. Maybe it's someone I knew in school. This is the high tourist season when Americans visit England."

"Well, that would be a nice surprise," Betty said.

As we left the ladies' room, I was trembling so hard I could barely hold the door for those behind me. A quick survey of the hallway, however, quieted my racing heart. Trevor was nowhere in sight. Perhaps it really had been an acquaintance from home, or someone who mistook me for a friend. The world, I reminded myself, is filled with doubles, many of them very nice and respectable people.

We purchased our tickets to the Roman Baths, the final three admitted to the assembled tour. Those behind us would have to wait for the next group to depart.

Assuring us that we were in for a treat, our guide began describing the discovery of the warm spring by the Romans who invaded and occupied Britain from the first through the fourth centuries A.D. As he led us through the series of rooms constructed to house the bathing facilities, he pointed out the dramatic engineering features the Romans used to build and maintain the baths. My heart stopped momentarily when he paused alongside the Great Bath to direct our attention upward to another tour group lining the terrace balustrade to view the alfresco pool, but Trevor was not among them.

"The water's green and icky." Dawn's whiny voice reflected the pout on her face.

"The water I drank in the Pump Room was perfectly clear," another member of our group said. "It must come from a different source."

The guide laughed. "Everyone notices the difference, but the water for the pump and the baths all come from the spring. It's actually clear and only appears to be green in the pool because of the algae growth."

He waited while everyone snapped photos, then herded us through the complex of bathing and dressing chambers into the museum. There he talked about the artifacts, statues, and stone fragments unearthed during archaeological digs. Some, he told us, were from the temple adjacent to the baths. Classic Roman in architectural style, the columned temple was of great importance to the centurions and their families stationed at the nearby fort during three centuries of occupation. Its large sacrificial altar was located outside the building so the public could participate in worship observances that involved the sacrifice of a cow, sheep, or pig to the goddess Sulis Minerva.

"Yuck!" Dawn's voice echoed across the hall.

"This is fascinating," Betty murmured, as we wandered past the exhibits that contained excavated objects ranging from coins, gemstones, jewelry, and candle holders to large fragments of inscribed stone altars and tombstones representing the kingdoms that utilized the waters after the barbarians overran the Romans.

Dawn expelled a loud sigh representing total boredom. Out of the corner of my eye, I studied Betty's face and wondered how soon she would abandon the effort to educate her daughter about Britain's history, cancel the itinerary of gardens and historic homes, and devote the bulk of their vacation to London, taking in the West End shows, the bargains on Oxford Street, and the glitz of Harrod's Department Store.

When everyone in the group finished contemplating the wonders of the museum and assembled behind the guide, he told us we would move on to the Roman Temple directly beneath the Pump Room, where the lecture portion of the tour would end. Just beyond was the museum shop where we could purchase mementos of our visit before exiting onto the street.

Slowed by Dawn's saunter, another outward display of her disinterest, Betty and I lagged behind the others. By the time we arrived in the Temple area, we were on the outer rim of the group assembled around the guide. I strained to hear his presentation. It was almost inaudible because of the din from the tour group that preceded ours, a talkative bunch who were slow to move on. To get closer to the guide, I ducked under the low archway separating us.

Just as I emerged on the far side, someone stepped from behind a pillar, grabbed my arm, and held on fast.

"Miss Tyler, I presume," he said. "Or may I call you Miss Morgan?"

CHAPTER THREE

Green Room Guests

Trevor! Why had I thought I could escape?

"You may not call me anything." My voice was little more than a whisper, but my fury was unmistakable.

"You're a scrappy one, aren't you?" The amusement in his eyes and on his lips was a beacon warning me that murderers derive great joy from taunting their victims before the final kill.

"And you're a wicked, wicked man," I said, unable to concoct a sensible response.

He stared at me for a long moment, tightening his grip on my arm. "Excuse me, my dear, but all I did was offer you a sip of my water. Not only did you refuse that courtesy, but you dumped both it and your stale coffee into my lap. If anyone is to be labeled wicked, your behavior is more deserving of that than mine."

I drew myself up to my full height. "That was an accident. If it had been anyone else, I would have apologized, but I don't apologize to criminals."

"What are you talking about?"

"The order you gave someone to kill that poor

girl, and..."

My response must have unnerved him because the hand that had gripped me flew to his mouth to stifle a nasty laugh. As the guide stopped talking and all eyes turned toward Trevor, I grabbed that opportunity to flee, sprinting across the Temple, up the stairway to the museum shop, and out the exit to the street filled with tourists. I ran as never before, dashing through the plaza, skirting knots of sightseers, clomping along the stone sidewalk past elderly ladies walking their dogs and young mothers pushing prams, heedless of approaching cars at the cross streets. Once again the pedestrian lights opposite the train station were in my favor. I mounted the stairs to the westbound tracks two at a time and reached the platform just as a train pulled in.

Panting, I ran toward the nearest uniformed trainman. "Is this train going to Bristol?"

"Right you are," he said.

Even if Trevor had followed me, I felt confident that I had put enough distance between us. Still, I was not content until the doors closed and we began to roll out of the Bath station.

Elspeth had been right. The journey to Bristol was under fifteen minutes, time to catch my breath and refocus on the talk show that now was a mere two hours away. Since I had no way of knowing whether Trevor would continue to Bristol after our encounter or head in a different direction, I decided to forsake plans to report him to the railway authorities. Cognizant that someone had uncovered his dastardly scheme, he could have escaped in any number of directions. Instead of sending the police on a useless chase, I hailed a cab outside the station and went directly to the television studio.

The assistant producer ushered me into her office with a friendly enough smile, although I sensed that her mind was cluttered with a dozen conflicting obligations.

"Terribly glad to meet you, Tara," she said. "I'm Phoebe. Are you familiar with our show, Sophia Plus Six?"

"No, I just flew in yesterday, so ..."

She did not wait for me to complete my sentence. "It makes no difference. You'll catch on right away. It's very free flowing. Off the top of the head sort of exchange. Great fun. You're our token American. Always like one in the mix. Keeps the conversation lively. So you write mysteries?"

"Actually only one, so far."

"Must be a winner to bring you here."

"I feel honored. The U.K. is the home of the world's greatest mystery writers."

She smiled blankly. "So I'm told. We're also number one in pop music and we have a spectacular artist on today's panel, Clyde Dale." She waited for my reaction.

"The name's familiar, but not as a pop star," I apologized, wondering what connection the celebrity had with brewery horses. I endeavored to erase the frown from Phoebe's face by adding, "Perhaps I'll recognize his music if he performs on the show."

She brightened. "Of course you will. He'll start off with something middle of the road from his latest CD, then Sophia Rydal, the panel moderator, will bring him over to the table and chat a bit before calling in the others. You'll enter one at a time, do your own thing for a few minutes. There's a monitor in the green room to follow along and a staff member will send each of you out at the right moment, so there's nothing to worry about."

"That relieves my mind," I said.

Phoebe, however, had more on hers. She leaned toward me and waved her forefinger in my face. "Now this is important. Clyde will close with a really rousing finale that's guaranteed to whip up the audience, so I want you to move with the beat at your seat, sing along, maybe get up and dance around, interact with the other guests. Whatever does it for you."

"I'll try my best. Just out of curiosity, who are the other guests?"

"Always a great, diverse group." She leafed through the papers on the desk until she located the program. "Sophia won't have enough time to cover all she'd like. In addition to Clyde, we have Gerald Melrose, who writes naughty things about the past and present Royals. There's Lucy Cox the Shakespearean actress, Sean Pool, who leads the Greenpeace sit-ins at nuclear plants around the world, and Evans of Evans and Rhys, those incredible creators of 'Torquaytoons.'"

I had never heard of anyone on the panel and could not imagine how she thought such a curious assortment would have enough in common to generate conversation throughout an hour-long show. Perhaps in the past I had been thrust into a more dismal situation, but none flew to mind. I smiled weakly and lied, "It sounds like great fun."

"Splendid. Then let's trot on over to makeup."

"Makeup?"

"Get a little color into your cheeks, emphasize your eyes, fluff up your hair."

My hand flew up to my hair automatically. The last time I glanced into a mirror it had seemed to be adequately fluffy, but perhaps television cameras had a tendency to make it appear squashed, much as they add several pounds to one's frame. Not understanding either the technology or Phoebe's agenda, I followed meekly as her strappy four-inch heels clicked down the hall to a veritable beauty salon.

"This is Tara," she told the stylist. "See what you can do with her, Raphael."

As Phoebe's precarious sandals clacked toward her next victim, I faced reality. She had left me to the devices of a man in a flaming henna ponytail wearing a smock over denim overalls with oversize cuffs that dragged across the floor. Combs, scissors, curling irons, and rollers cluttered the counter next to the basin where he was testing water temperature.

Raphael's critical eye assessed my hair. "When did you shampoo last, Precious?"

"This morning," I told him, feeling more than a little snappish.

"You've been in the wind since then, I can tell. Let's give it some body." So saying, he reached for a bottle containing a yellow cream, poured a glob into his palm, and began working it into my hair. "This is fabulous," he said, as he saturated each strand with the unknown quantity.

"What is it?"

"My secret formula, Precious. You can buy it at better stores." I vowed to do no such thing as he twirled me around in the chair to assess his work. "See how gorgeous you look. Now let's give you a glow with some darker foundation and a rosy tint. Close your eyes." He applied several substances to my face, audibly praising his handiwork with each stroke. "Last, but not least, those fabulous eyes." So saying, he dunked a brush into a pot of color and stroked it across my lids. A layer of mascara on my lashes added the finishing touch. "You look amazing."

He rotated my chair so I could apprise myself in the mirror. The stranger staring back was a refugee from an MTV video. She sported spiked hair, makeup so thick a fingernail could scour a message across her forehead, and lampshade fringes framing her eyes. "I'm sorry, but this won't do," I complained. "I don't look like this. Not ever."

"Precious, the word is that you're a mystery writer, but you didn't look like one when you came through that door. This conveys the right message. You do want to sell your books, don't you?"

"Yes, but…"

"There you are. The medium is the message. You look gloriously mysterious. Everyone will want to rush out and buy a copy of your book."

"I'm sure you mean well, but I'd like this toned down before I go on stage. I'll be embarrassed beyond words."

"When you hear the reaction of the audience, you'll realize that I know exactly what I'm doing." He did not wait for my reply, but removed the plastic cape protecting my proper navy suit, brushed stray hairs from my shoulders, and pulled me to my feet. "Here's Angie, come to take you to the green room. Doesn't she look gorgeous, Angie?"

Angie grinned. I could not tell if she agreed with Raphael or wore a perpetual smirk. "Follow me, please," she said, and I obeyed.

I was the first to arrive in the green room, a casual area with chairs and sofas sporting pillows so plump they occupied most of the seating space. They were flanked by reading lamps, tables cluttered with current magazines and newspapers, and one holding modest snacks. The far wall housed several television monitors flickering with images of the show presently on the air. The volume was turned low, but there was no mistaking the splendor of the rose garden captured by the camera. In the foreground, a man in mud-caked Wellingtons leaned on a hoe as he shared professional tips with viewers.

I chose a magazine from the pile before me and had begun leafing through it when someone bounded through the door.

"I can't believe these people. Didn't they feed you either?" A small, wiry man stood with hands on hips. Hairless, save for a goatee, he wore a yellow jump suit, yellow and black checkered cape, and red boots.

"Nobody asked, and I'm not hungry anyway, but you might try the bowl of chips over there," I said, pointing to a table against the wall.

"Not exactly the ticket for an empty stomach," he

said, as he snatched a handful and stuffed them into his mouth. "Besides, they're loaded with oil and salt, all wrong for my health regimen." His disdain did not deter him from helping himself again. Four fistfuls later, he appropriated the entire bowl and plopped himself on the sofa opposite. "Sure you won't have some?"

"No, thanks. I had a lovely lunch at the Pump Room."

He whooped. "Don't tell me you're a tourist. Nobody goes there but tourists."

"Yes, you could call me a tourist. This is my first real trip to Great Britain, so I'll make the usual rounds and gawk properly."

"Am I to assume that you're sitting here as a fan or as a friend of a staff member?"

"Neither. I'm going to be on some kind of a panel. I gather by your costume…"

"Costume?" He threw back his head and laughed. "Sweetheart, this is the very latest and it cost me dearly. Am I in style? Decidedly. Am I wearing a costume? Don't dare let my designer hear you say that. She'll have your scalp. And I strongly suspect that you and I are on the same panel. So, are you an actress?"

"No, I write."

"Anything I might have read?"

"Probably not. It's a mystery about a murder that took place in the United States last century. My editor sent me over here to promote it."

I felt his sharp eyes appraising me. "Yes, I see that you do have a mysterious air about you."

My hands flew to my head. "Oh, if it's the hair, please don't judge me by this horrible style. Raphael in makeup filled it with some kind of goop that I plan to wash out when I shower tonight. In fact, if I had a mirror, I'd try to put it back to normal before the show."

"Ask and ye shall receive," he said, reaching into one of his huge pockets and extracting a small mirror. "I'll hold it while you do whatever it is you have to do, but let me assure you that you have the certain something that television cameras love."

"You're very kind. Still, I won't feel like myself until I can flatten down the spikes he fashioned. My hair looks as if it's never been combed."

"That's the style, Sweetheart," he said, patiently holding the mirror while I labored to undo Raphael's mistake. "Don't you want to look trendy?"

"Not if trendy means messy," I grumbled, managing to tame my errant mane just as another guest arrived.

A middle-aged man, he wore the obligatory Scottish tweeds befitting his distinguished air, a jacket with padded leather elbows that screamed old wealth. I concluded at once that he must be Gerald Melrose, chronicler of the Royals.

He extended his hand to my companion. "Ah, Virgie. We meet again."

"Greetings, Gerry. Those sideburns of yours are growing grayer." Clearly old friends, they shook hands warmly.

"Wait a minute." I pointed at Virgil. "I thought you were Clydesdale."

Both men laughed aloud. Virgil shook his head. "Dearie, you are something else. Virgil Mankowitz is not the kind of name that sells records, so my manager changed it to Clyde Dale."

"That's what I said. Like the horses."

Virgil laughed again. "Almost, but without the 's' in the middle. You see the reasoning involved, surely. Give the public some kind of connection, a name that they remember from somewhere else. The singer Englebert Humperdinck took his name from the 19th Century composer, and Tom Jones took his from the title of a novel. As you put it so bluntly, mine brings to mind a breed of workhorse. What does that make me?"

I colored. "It must make you a powerful competitor in the rock music business."

"That he is, that he is," Gerald said, settling himself in an easy chair. "And whom might you be, my dear?"

"Sarah Morgan, but my editor thought I needed a name change, too, so I'm going by Tara Tyler during my book tour."

"Splendid. Then that's what we shall call you. Tell me, Tara, is this your first talk show?"

"Yes, it is, and I don't mind confessing that I'm scared stiff."

"There's nothing to be afraid of," Virgil said. "Sophia is a smashing hostess. She moves the conversation along with provocative questions for the panelists and we banter back and forth madly. The time is up before you know it."

"Hi, everyone. We've almost reached the full complement. Evans is the only missing link." Angie stood in the doorway ushering in a woman approaching mid-life and a tousled young man in sweats and sneakers.

Introductions all around confirmed my initial suspicion that the woman with uncommon stage presence was Lucy Cox, the Shakespearean actress, and her companion, Sean Pool, had come direct from a strenuous sit-in. Both wore the unmistakable burnt orange shade of makeup that Raphael touted.

"Evans does plan to be here, doesn't he?" Gerald looked concerned.

"He should be coming along any minute. He rang up not long ago to say he was detained by a crazy lady on the train."

Gerald laughed heartily. "If I know him, he'll work that into his next episode and have a splendid story for us today, besides." He cocked an eye at me. "Evans is one of the wittiest men I've ever met, always a delight, just like his satiric look at life with the semi-upper crust. Are you familiar with 'Torquaytoons?'"

I shook my head and said nothing, for at that precise moment, the door opened and Trevor entered.

CHAPTER FOUR

Television Talk Show

"Well, hello there," he said, looking directly at me, a Cheshire cat grin on his face. "I've been waiting for this moment."

"You're not....You can't be...Can you...?" I squeaked.

Gerald rose from his chair and hurried over to pump Trevor's hand. "Evans, this is a pleasure. I was just telling the young lady here what a wit you are."

Trevor threw back his head and laughed. "It's good to have someone of authority on my side. For a second, I thought she was going to attack me again."

All eyes in the room rotated to me. "Your name is Evans? I thought it was Trevor."

"So it is. Trevor Evans at your service, Miss Morgan. I'm delighted to see you again under less stressful conditions. However I suggest that the next time you listen in on a private conversation you curb those wild conclusions."

Virgil perked up, sensing an altercation. "What's he talking about?"

Trevor gave a wicked laugh as he settled himself on the couch next to me. Instinctively, I flinched and edged away. He, however, seemed to be enjoying himself. "Miss Morgan and I met quite abruptly on the train when she took it upon herself to misinterpret my end of a phone conversation with Tom about one of our characters."

I felt my face turning all shades of red beneath my orange greasepaint. "A character? I had no idea. I'm so embarrassed. I thought that you…"

He finished my admission. "She thought I was a murderer, folks, and proceeded to dump her coffee on me."

The hearty laughter all around drowned out my whispered apology. "I'm terribly sorry. Did I ruin your suit? Please let me pay to have it cleaned."

The amusement in his eyes spilled over into a huge grin, and it struck me that Dawn's assessment of him had been right on the money. "Miss Morgan, the suit is renewable, but making contact with you has been the experience of a lifetime."

I had never felt so uncomfortable or so foolish. "You're very kind, Mr. Evans. But seriously, how can I make it up to you?"

"We'll begin with dinner right after the show. And I expect you to address me by my given name. I'm Trevor to you, not Mr. Evans."

I stared at him. My voice refused to function.

"Good. That's settled then, provided I can call you Sarah. Or do you prefer Tara?"

I blushed. "Sarah, please. Tara's a bit too exotic for my blood."

"Oh, I don't know about that. You look a lot more

exotic now than you did on the train, not that it's an improvement. What have they done to you?"

The ice broken, I shared his laughter. "Isn't it dreadful? Raphael wanted to make me look mysterious."

"Raphael?"

"The makeup man."

He nodded, understanding. "There's one waiting in the wings at every television studio. I pretend I don't hear when the producer points me in that direction."

"I wish I could be that independent."

"From what I've seen, you're one of the most independent women I've ever met."

I blushed again. "That's something I'd like to forget."

He leaned into me and spoke so softly that the others could not hear him. "Tell me that on our fiftieth wedding anniversary."

Stunned, I pretended I hadn't understood, and directed my attention to Sean, who was answering Gerald's question about his latest Greenpeace escapade. As Sean elaborated, Trevor fell silent, but I was so strongly aware of his presence at my elbow that I was unable to focus on anything else. At length I heard him give a short laugh, and when I glanced over at him, he was shaking his head and smiling at me apologetically.

"I can't imagine whatever possessed me to say that," he said. "Ordinarily, I'm perfectly capable of bottling up my subconscious thoughts until I find the perfect outlet through one of my cartoon characters."

"I'm sorry I'm not familiar with your cartoons. Gerald thinks the world of them."

He smiled appreciatively. "They've become more

popular than I ever dreamed, but it's a ticklish job keeping the story line current and the characters appealing. Gussie Glam has been getting on my nerves of late because there's just so much comedy you can extract from a selfish matron whose idea of a good time is getting Botox injections and tummy tucks. I decided that her early demise would blast the futility of trying to stay young through cosmetic surgery while the years tick away. The conversation you overheard was an exploration of ways to ax her from the story and also make a point."

"If only I'd known. I was planning to report you to the rail authorities and have you picked up on suspicion of murder."

He roared with laughter. "You were? Tom will love this story."

"Tom?"

"Tom Rhys, my partner. We spend most of our working hours thrashing out plots and analyzing character. If we can't be together in the office, we make contact however we can, most often by mobile, the cause of this morning's misunderstanding."

"Being a perfect klutz with crayons since kindergarten, I should think that the hardest part of your job would be the art work."

"Actually, it's the easiest part because once we develop a plot and sketch out a character in our minds, we can reproduce it in seconds on the sketch pad. Now that computers do the bulk of the work, we have the process of drawing each action frame down to a science. The voice-overs and the soundtrack are done in our studio against the completed film."

"It never occurred to me that I was privy to a brainstorming session."

His smile sent shivers up my back. Abstractly, I wondered why I was drawn to a man who only hours before had filled me with terror. "Well, Sarah, you shall be our guest at the very disheveled London office where the 'Torquaytoons' are born and the studio where England's finest actors bring them to life. Lucy, by the way, is the voice of Dame Clarinda. Lucy, can you do a little bit of Clarinda to give Sarah some idea of the character?"

Lucy, whose demeanor suggested years of treading the boards and mastering complex heroines from Greek tragedies to the experimental plays of modern minimalists, obliged by hitching herself to the edge of her chair and affecting a pose typical of an elderly lady from old money. She spoke in a throaty voice that had been bathed with more than its share of cigarette smoke. "My deahs, I'll have you know that the Queen herself admired my hat the last time I dined at St. James's which, I'm certain you recall, is the exclusive restaurant on the sixth floor of Fortnam and Mason's. She was charming, as always, and hardly looks her age, although I must say that she might have chosen a more becoming outfit. Yellow is not her color, especially against her pale complexion and gray hair."

After acknowledging the smiles and applause from the others, Lucy explained her character to me. "Clarinda is overbearing. At the same time, she's quite pathetic because she gathers most of her stories from the tabloids and twists them into fabrications to enhance her own importance. She's a recurring character who often launches a new episode as she slurps her tea and spills crumpet crumbs into her lap while relating the latest gossip. She and her lady friends regularly lunch at a decaying hotel that once was the most prestigious resort in Torquay. Does that give you some insight into her?"

"Yes, your voice gives her exactly the right balance that suggests fading aristocracy, somewhere on the road from onetime snob to social has-been. But what is Torquay?"

"Sorry. It didn't occur to me that you wouldn't know," Trevor said. "Torquay is a resort in Devon. It's known as the English Riviera because the mild climate draws the wealthy, or would-be wealthy. It's very picturesque with palm trees and tropical vegetation and a beautiful sandy beach, but a clientele that's becoming somewhat frayed at the edges. Our characters represent the variety of tourists who go there for one reason or another, from minor Royals to confidence tricksters."

"Do you base them on people you've known, or are they're drawn strictly from your imagination?"

"Actually, I discover them wherever I go, in pubs, on trains, the Underground. The U.K. is blessed with a brilliant mixture of personalities and body types."

"He nails them from the get-go," Virgil said, rising in response to a signal from Phoebe. Before reaching the door, he added, "I almost hesitate to flatter Evans because his show airs Saturday evenings and it's so popular that people stay home in droves to see it instead of coming out to the theater and concerts."

Trevor grinned, "They always have the option of

recording 'Torquaytoons.' I'd hate to think that I'm the cause of a declining live theater audience."

"'Torquaytoons' sounds like fun," I told him.

"It is, but not nearly so much fun as running into you."

I blushed again and my stomach churned inexplicably.

Overlooking my silence, he continued, "When you go home, I'll send along tapes so you can follow the series from the beginning at your leisure."

"I'd like that. How long has the show been on the air?"

"Three years so far, and we've been renewed for at least one more. It helps pay the rent."

"I should think so. You live in London?"

"Yes, ever since we've been on the telly, but I always jump at the opportunity to go home, which is where I'm headed this evening."

I hesitated. "Is your home in Pembrokeshire?"

He chuckled. "You know more about me that I know about you, Miss Sarah, Tara, or whomever you choose to be, thanks to a pair of sharp ears. Yes, I grew up there and my Mum and brother and his family are there. Why do you ask?"

Just then, Virgil appeared on the monitor in the company of a bedazzling blond speaking into the camera. She, I realized, was Sophia Rydal, the hostess. Gerald rose from his chair to turn up the volume just in time to hear her welcome viewers to a show that she promised would be, "…fabulous, my dears, following an opening number by everyone's favorite rock artist, Clyde Dale."

Sensing that further conversation would disorient the others waiting for their own entrance cues, I whispered to Trevor, "I'll explain about Pembrokeshire later."

"All the more reason why I can't wait until dinner," he said, with a smile that curled my toes.

Virgil sat down to play a piece I had never before heard. He was backed by a small combo with an extraordinarily noisy percussionist and amplification that must have been off the scale.

Trevor laughed when I put my hands to my ears. "Not your favorite style of music?"

I shook my head.

"Nor mine," he said. "That's something else you and I have in common."

The others in the studio audience, however, must have loved that rendition because they gave Virgil a standing ovation that lasted longer, I gathered, than the stage manager liked. One of the monitors before us captured him motioning Sophia to begin questioning her guest even before he smoothed his checkered cape and settled into the seat next to hers. As soon as they began chatting, Phoebe returned and motioned Gerald to follow her to the wings and await his entrance.

One by one, my green room companions were summoned until Trevor's departure left me alone. I wanted to linger long enough to hear his conversation with Sophia, but Phoebe hustled me out to the wings and into a chair across from a silent monitor. I could not read Trevor's lips, but knew he was uproariously funny; the camera zoomed in on audience members laughing so hard they were crying.

Angie, standing nearby, leaned over and said, "He's the funniest man I've ever met. I'm mad about 'Torquaytoons.'"

"I'm told it's wonderful," I murmured.

She regarded me with disbelief, as if I came from another planet. "You've never seen it?"

"No, but Trevor promised to give me some tapes."

"You'll see what you've been missing," she said, with a modicum of pity.

He must have made another side-splitting remark because the camera turned once more to the audience, now screaming with delight. As it panned across the auditorium, I did a double-take, for among those seated in the second row were two women laughing so hard they clutched each other to keep from rolling into the aisle.

Angie pointed to them. "Look at those people. That's the typical reaction every time he's on the show. He really increases our ratings."

I was hardly listening to her, so astounded was I to see Betty and Dawn Ambler. Before I could sort out how they might have reached the studio, Angie took me by the arm and escorted me to the curtain separating us from the stage. "You're on," she said, and shoved me through the passageway.

"Everyone please welcome Tara Tyler, author of *The Rittenhouse Murder*," Sophia cried as she beckoned me into the nearest chair.

The next few minutes were dizzying. Afterward, I recalled that we chatted briefly about my book before she tossed out several topics for discussion by the panel. They responded eagerly, interrupting one another often with clever asides that guaranteed continual laughter rippling throughout the audience. It struck me that Sophia was asking generic questions that might be asked of a comparable panel, so glib and rehearsed were the answers. No matter, everyone, including those on stage, appeared to be having a grand time. As the only flustered participant, I dreaded appearing foolish, so I spoke only when addressed and refrained from offering opinions that others might regard as banal.

The grand finale arrived not a moment too soon. His cape flying, Virgil leaped from his chair onto the piano bench and began pounding the keys in a frenzy. The guitarist strummed his instrument so hard I thought the nails would be ripped from his fingers, and the drummer put on a show that propelled listeners to their feet. Clapping in time to the music, some even dancing in the aisles, the audience sang along to lyrics that seemed to me little more than monosyllabic nonsense. Clearly, I had been out of the mainstream for a very long time.

For the first few bars, I remained seated, yearning to crawl under the discussion table, until Trevor, grinning, grabbed my arm and coaxed me from my seat. As he swung me around the stage in time to the music, I saw that the others also were obeying Phoebe's directive. Gerald and Lucy twirled together in formal ballroom-like fashion, while Sean and Sophia linked arms and gyrated near her microphone.

"Hang in there for another minute or so," Trevor

shouted into my ear. "He'll play until he drops from exhaustion, but we can stop when the camera cuts out."

"You've been in this situation before?"

He laughed and drew me closer. "Are you talking about television shows?"

"Of course. What did you think?"

"With you, I intend to keep all options open."

CHAPTER FIVE

The Bold Proposition

Trevor's impudent smile flustered me even more than the statement I was still trying to interpret. My effort to remain impassive succeeded until the stage manager signaled the end of the show and I became the recipient of a huge hug. When I caught my breath, I demanded, "What's that for?"

His eyes teased. "That's for being a brave woman and making it to the end of your first television talk show unscathed. One down, more to go than you probably want to think about right now."

"That's the truth." I stepped backward with exaggerated decorum. It would not do to let him suspect that I had enjoyed every second in his arms.

His answer was lost in the din of audience members mounting the stage to seek autographs. The first wave brought Dawn and Betty doling out more hugs.

"How cool," Dawn said.

"Dawn's so impressed," Betty whispered in my ear. "I don't know what I'd done if we hadn't met you two."

"We two? Then you've already met Trevor Evans?"

"Oh yes. He's terribly nice. Right after you ran out of the Roman Baths, he recognized Dawn, so we began talking and he explained that you and he were both scheduled to appear on this program, but that you had some kind of a crazy notion about him he didn't understand. He invited us to come along with him to the show and of course Dawn was thrilled. She'd taken a fancy to him right away, and when she learned that he's famous, she was ecstatic."

"It's a long, ridiculous story," I said. "I had no idea who he was, so when I overheard him on the train plotting a murder of one of his characters, I naturally thought he was about to commit a real one. When he found me in Bath, I was terrified. That's why I ran away without saying goodbye to you."

Trevor had been listening to us, grinning from ear to ear. "Now I ask you, Betty, do I look vicious?"

She laughed. "Anything but. We couldn't imagine why Sarah left so abruptly, but it all worked out beautifully. Dawn's having the time of her life. Look at that, would you." She pointed to the teenager who had zeroed in on the combo and already was perched on the piano bench next to Virgil and chatting with the drummer. "Meeting a famous rock star is bound to be the highlight of our trip for her. For myself, I wouldn't mind meeting Lucy Cox. She was marvelous in that film about Mary, Queen of Scots we saw last year."

Trevor appropriated her arm. "Come with me and I'll introduce you." Seeing me hesitate, he reached back and grabbed my hand. "You're coming along, too, young lady. Don't even think about running away again. We haven't begun to talk."

I followed meekly. Could it be that my usually sensible self was succumbing to the charms of a man who only a few hours earlier I had regarded as a demon?

Trevor retained a commanding grip on my hand as he introduced Betty to Lucy, Sophia, Gerald, and Sean. He even handed Betty's camera to one of the cameramen and persuaded him to snap poses of Betty with Lucy, Dawn with Virgil's combo, and both of them flanked by all the panelists, preserving memories they would not soon forget.

"You're so very kind," Betty told him. "This afternoon has been beyond our wildest dreams."

"Mine, too," he said, tossing me a wink and squeezing my hand.

By the time Betty and I exchanged addresses and contact numbers in England, the cast and crew had cleared the stage and Dawn, aglow, was clutching Virgil's latest CDs to her chest, items he just happened to have brought along.

"I think I like England, after all," she said.

"I'm glad we've been able to reverse your opinion," Trevor told her. "When you get to London, let me know. I'll give you and your mother a tour of our studio."

She gazed at him, starry-eyed. "Ooh, that would be so cool!"

As they left, Trevor turned to me. "Her youthful enthusiasm is easy for me to understand because I'm always impressed by people who have made it in the entertainment industry."

I knew my aloof exterior had crumbled when an involuntary compliment popped out of my mouth. "You should include yourself among them. From all accounts, your cartoon is a national hit."

"So they tell me, but I'd appreciate your input once you have a chance to evaluate the tapes. You seem like the sort of person who recognizes quality and refuses to be influenced by popularity polls."

"I'll look forward to seeing them. I'm sorry, though, that I couldn't hear what you were saying on the show that tickled everyone so."

"You'll have that opportunity next week when the show is aired."

"Next week? But I thought…"

"You thought it was live? No, shows like this are always taped."

"So I didn't miss anything after all?"

"Only the commercials. You'll even be able to see how Raphael's imagination plays in close-up shots."

"You just brought me down to earth with a thud. Do I have time to scrape some of this gook off my face?"

"I'll grant you all the time you need since I can't afford taking you out into public looking like a lady of the evening. I'm known as a pretty conservative guy, and any hint that I've kicked over the traces would end up in tabloid headlines."

I studied his face with a mixture of amusement and admiration. "You handle celebrity very well."

He steered me toward the dressing room with a firm hand. "Sarah, it's very important to me that you do not regard me as a celebrity. Only the characters in my cartoons have that honor. I'm strictly a country boy who makes his living in the big city doing what he does best and loving every minute of it. Especially minutes like this. Now get in there and clean yourself up."

I left him laughing as I hurried into the dressing room to scrub the greasepaint from my face and right most of the wrong that Raphael had committed.

Two hours later, we were topping off a delicious dinner of Dover sole with queen of puddings, an airy, meringue-enveloped concoction that might have been whipped together by angels. Throughout the meal, Trevor had regaled me with amusing anecdotes taken from his cartoons and his real life experiences in battling traditional television programming. His fresh sense of humor bowled me over. It was easy to understand the success of 'Torquaytoons' and its appeal to viewers at large. As the waiter poured our after-dinner coffee, I felt happy, even giddy. Within a few short hours, Trevor had upended all my apprehensions about the book tour. Now I was eager to continue, especially if running into him again figured into the schedule. To my dismay, the barriers I so often erected between myself and casual acquaintances were tumbling decisively, clearing the way for me to fall unabashedly in love. I clung to his every word, chastising myself for my naiveté, yet incapable of backing away.

"I've talked more than my share," he said, jerking me back to the present. "Now it's about time you tell me your connection with Pembrokeshire. Did your family originate there?"

"I'm not sure where my ancestors lived, only that it was somewhere in Wales. They emigrated to the colonies so long ago that the generations along the way forgot the reasons, only that they came from a beautiful spot."

"That could be any place in Wales," Trevor said. "It's all beautiful. You'll see. So what piqued your interest in Pembrokeshire?"

"The disappearances."

In one brief second, his sunny expression disappeared, as if a black cloud had descended about his shoulders. Pain shot up my arm as he grabbed my wrist. "What are you talking about?"

I shivered. Had I overstepped an invisible boundary?

"Yes? Go on," he prodded me.

"Perhaps I'm on the wrong track…?"

"Let me be the judge."

I swallowed before plunging into the unknown. "Not long ago, I read about a number of young women who disappeared while walking along a coastal pathway. The newspapers said that the bodies were never found, so it's not known if they ran away, committed suicide, or were murdered."

"And…?"

My voice was low, yet firm. "I think they were murdered."

His eyes seemed to pierce through mine. "And how do you propose to prove or disprove your theory?"

"I thought it might be worthwhile to investigate the victims' backgrounds and explore the area."

"For a book?"

I nodded.

He took a long, deep breath. "I see. Have you made definite plans to go there?"

"No, not yet. I'm due back in London on Monday, so Elspeth – the woman who's arranging my tour here – made reservations for me at a hotel in Cardiff for this weekend. She said I should get my feet wet in Wales and that the Cardiff Castle and the Museum of Welsh Life in St. Fagans are good places to start."

" For the typical tourist, they are, but Cardiff is little more than a continuation of England with a dollop of Welsh sauce on top. To find the answers you seek, you need to go directly to Pembrokeshire."

"I intend to at the first opportunity. For starters, I thought that someone at the hotel in Cardiff could suggest places in Pembrokeshire where I might stay, and perhaps the name of a local newspaper editor who could give me the background of some of the girls. I can't shake the feeling that they must have left clues others have overlooked."

"Forget the hotel in Cardiff. You're looking at your best source."

"You?" My head began to swirl. For a moment, my instincts retreated to those that had overwhelmed me earlier in the day. Trevor could not possibly have been involved in the disappearances. Or could he? I plunged in defiantly. "Why are you my best source?"

"As they say in real estate, location, location, location."

"What do you mean?"

"I'll explain after I present my proposition."

My eyes widened. "Proposition?"

His smile came readily. "It's nothing scandalous, Sarah, merely practical. My mother owns three cottages adjacent to the coastal path all within a short distance of each other. She lives in the family home where I grew up and where I stay when I go back to visit. My brother and his wife live in the second cottage, and the third is rented out by the day, the week, or seasonally. If nobody has booked it for this weekend, it's all yours."

The troubling suspicions I harbored moments earlier fled into the sunset. I considered Trevor's proposition for less than five seconds. "How can we find out if it's available?"

"You're interested? Good. I'll phone home as soon as I settle up with the waiter."

Minutes later, we were standing by the Floating Harbor where John Cabot set sail for the New World and, a century later, the London Company launched adventurers to colonize Virginia. Now I was an explorer like them, venturing off to an unknown land.

Trevor had retrieved his mobile phone and was about to call when I located mine in the depths of my purse. "Wait a minute. Before you talk with your mother, I'd better call Elspeth to make sure it's all right with her."

He laughed. "Checking up on my reputation? A single woman in a strange land can't be too careful. Go ahead, if it makes you feel better."

I blushed. "That's not exactly the reason."

"Excuses aren't necessary, Sarah. I'll walk away and keep my distance while you chat with her."

"Don't be silly. Besides, I need you nearby to

explain to her exactly where she can locate me. That is, if the cottage is available and she can cancel my reservation in Cardiff."

Elspeth answered on the second ring and spent the first few minutes questioning me about the telecast. When I managed to sneak in the fact that Trevor had invited me to stay in Pembrokeshire for the weekend, she screamed so loudly I had to hold the phone away from my ear. "Sarah Tara, every woman in Britain has her eye on him, and to think you've captured his heart in one afternoon."

"No, no, it's nothing like that, Elspeth. This is strictly a business arrangement. He'll show me around Pembrokeshire and help me find contacts for my next book."

She refused to accept my mundane excuse. "I expect to see you two in the tabloids within the next week. Don't disappoint me."

I was thankful that Trevor was only privy to my side of the conversation. Promising Elspeth that I'd call back in the event the cottage was not available, I instructed her to cancel the Cardiff hotel reservation if she didn't hear from me within five minutes. Then I relayed the address and phone number where she could find me in an emergency and agreed to contact her the minute I returned to London.

Trevor's call to his mother went through without a hitch; within moments I had a guaranteed reservation at her cottage. "That does it." He tucked the phone into his breast pocket and commandeered my overnight case. "Meredith is meeting us at Swansea."

"Meredith?"

"My brother. We have just enough time to catch the next train due at Bristol Parkway if the taxi I see coming our way needs a fare."

It did, and we made the train with a few minutes to spare. This time, we sat side by side, our shoulders touching and heads bent close in animated conversation. A casual observer might have imagined us to be very old friends. Perhaps even lovers?

CHAPTER SIX

Journey to Pembrokeshire

Meredith hailed us as we stepped onto the train platform at Swansea. A brawny, handsome man, he sported a jovial laugh and sufficient resemblance to Trevor that denying their relationship would have been out of the question. His voice was nearly identical to that of his brother except for an unfamiliar accent I could not readily place.

Introductions aside, Meredith took my arm and led me to his car, a serviceable Vauxhall, while Trevor followed close behind with my bag. "You'll have to stop by first thing tomorrow to meet Enid," he said. "When it's too cold and rainy to go out, I can always find her curled up reading a mystery, so talking with you will be a real treat for her."

"Enid is your wife?"

"That she is, the light of my life. You'll like her. I can tell you'll fit right into the family."

I froze. "Oh, but you have the wrong idea. Trevor and I aren't…we just met this morning and certainly don't plan…"

His laugh was deep and hearty. "I don't think I

owe you an apology, Sarah. I saw the way he looks at you. The men in our family don't bring young ladies home unless we have honorable intentions. I know Trevor like a book, and I can assure you he won't deviate from tradition, even if he does live in London most of the time. Now you might not have any idea what's churning around in the back of his mind, but I can assure you that he's mapping out your future even as we speak."

I was still thrashing around for a suitable response when we reached his car. Trevor came up from behind and said, "I'll toss these bags in the boot."

"You'll what?"

He grinned. "Sorry. That's the English language for you. Over here, what you call the trunk is the boot. And that's not the only linguistic quirk you'll run into." He said something to Meredith that was impossible to decipher, and both men chuckled at my puzzlement. "It's not mumbo-jumbo, Sarah. Simply an archaic language known as Welsh."

"Not so archaic," Meredith countered. "At least not in this part of the world."

"He's right," Trevor said, helping me into the back seat. "Following World War II, English became the dominant language of Wales. While we were growing up, Welsh was spoken only by the older generation. Purists became afraid it would disappear, so a national movement was begun to teach Welsh to all the school children. Consequently, every adult in western Wales is fluent today in both Welsh and English. It's very common to hear it spoken exclusively in some communities, but very few residents of Cardiff and

Swansea or any of the border towns speak or understand it."

"It sounds like no other language I've heard."

"A very good observation," Meredith said, taking command of the steering wheel. "Welsh is an ancient Celtic language, but quite distinct from Irish, Manx, and Gaelic. It's probably most closely related to Breton and Cornish. As children, we had no trouble picking it up, but I'm told by adults trying to master it, even those with several languages under their belt, that they're often stumped by the vocabulary and pronunciation. It has little or no relationship to anything they know."

I frowned. "Will I have trouble making myself understood here?"

Trevor tossed me an assuring smile. "Not at all. Folks here like to show their patriotism by opening all conversations with a few words of Welsh, but the shopkeepers are extremely practical and know that most of their customers speak English. Wherever you go, simply break the ice by saying, '*Bore da*,' meaning 'good morning' or 'good afternoon,' and follow that with whatever you need to say in English."

As we pulled out of the parking lot, Meredith pointed to a highway sign bearing the red Welsh dragon imprinted with destinations in both English and Welsh. "The dual language system on public signs is more of a tourism gimmick on the main highways, but it's extremely useful in rural areas where Welsh is the primary language of the older folks. And of course in my work, I'm never away from it like Trevor is. Even though we publish in English, many articles contain

Welsh phrases or words. I use both languages every day."

"Then that must be why I noticed a slight accent. What kind of work do you do, Meredith?"

"I'm the editor of the *Western Telegraph and Cymric Times.*"

When my voice returned, I said, "You're joking."

Trevor savored my astonishment. "No joke by a mile. Exactly what the lady requested, an editor with knowledge of the disappearances."

"Can I believe my good fortune?"

"Believe with all your heart. The Evans brothers are at your beck and command."

"If I didn't know better, I'd suspect there's magic afoot. I expected to spend several days tracking down the basics."

"And now it's being handed to you, no questions asked. Meredith's office is in Haverfordwest, the largest city in Pembrokeshire. You can be sure that he'll give you free rein of his files."

Meredith glanced back at me over his shoulder with an expression bordering on relief. "I expect you to take advantage of the offer first thing tomorrow, Sarah. Whatever you can unearth will put a lot of minds at rest."

"So it's settled," Trevor said, folding his arms. He lounged comfortably in the passenger seat, seemingly unperturbed that his brother was tooling down the M-4 motorway at a speed that would have rated me a ticket at home, and yet our car was crawling compared with those whooshing past us.

I moved to tighten my seat belt. "Are there no

speed limits here?"

"Only to the extent that drivers keep their limitations in mind," Trevor said. "Cars here are a great deal smaller than they are in Germany where the autobahns are built for muscle. Our cars can't take that kind of pounding, and since their price is very dear for most people, nobody deliberately tries to burn up the road and their investment along with it."

"I'm glad someone else is driving," I said. "Between the speed and navigating on what to me is the opposite side of the road, I'd end up in a ditch."

"You'll get used to it in no time," Meredith said, in a tone that suggested I was considering relocating to Wales. As if reading my mind, Trevor tossed me a smile that seemed to confirm that possibility in my future.

Minutes later, the M-4 ended and Meredith turned onto a local road that swooped and dipped between mist-shrouded hillocks. I might have been entering a new dimension. The landscape rolled seductively toward the west, dotted with quaint villages and stone farmhouses ancient in origin, yet sparkling with fresh paint, their gardens and gates adorned with roses of cabbage proportions. Thick, high hedges separated the farms to discourage the prolific flocks of sheep from roaming.

I took a deep breath, soaking in our surroundings. "You were right, Trevor. This countryside is stunning."

He looked pleased. "I thought you'd be impressed. It's particularly beautiful this time of the year when days are long. On clear evenings during the six weeks just before and after the summer solstice, you can sit outside and read until nearly midnight. See, it's already well past nine and there's still no need for headlights."

Meredith laughed. "We make up for that pleasure during winter, though. The sun goes down in the middle of the afternoon."

Just outside the village of Carmarthen, Trevor directed my attention to a mountain off to the right. "A little bit earlier, you mentioned magic, Sarah. If you're a believer, this is where you'll find Merlin's cave and burial mound."

"Merlin of King Arthur fame? Did he really exist?"

"So says tradition," Meredith said. "He's a key element of Welsh history, whether or not he really existed. Ask any Welshman and he'll swear that Merlin is the force behind his good luck."

"Meredith and I made the climb when we were youngsters and actually found a cave that must have been there for thousands of years, since the last glaciation," Trevor said. "It was isolated and mysterious enough to have belonged to a magician. There's also a well nearby that's been associated with Merlin, and a burial mound on the crest of the hill. Since nobody knows who actually lies there, the honor goes to him."

Even as I gazed toward the mountain, it faded from sight, enveloped by the evening mist. "This is a fairytale kind of place."

"The first of many you'll see in Wales," Trevor promised.

The sky, still eerily bright, was reflected in the

waters of Cardigan Bay when Meredith dropped us off before a stone cottage. Perched on a promenade alongside an inlet, it's windows mirrored the sinking sun. Trevor helped me from the car into a stiff breeze laced with briny salt air.

"This is a beautiful setting," I said. "Is this where I'll be staying?"

He retrieved my bag from the trunk. "We're almost there. This is our mother's home. I'll introduce you and she'll give you the key to the guest cottage. It's not far."

The pathway to the front door was lined with rose bushes, their blossoms ranging in hue from white to garnet. "Somebody must work full time to raise such enormous roses," I said.

"You'd think so, but they actually need very little care because of all the rain. Next to the daffodil, the national flower, roses are the most prolific bloom in Wales."

Even before we mounted the threshold, the door was opened by a slim, attractive middle-aged woman with piercing eyes of deep blue. She was the image of Trevor and Meredith.

Trevor propelled me forward gently. "Mum, this is Sarah Morgan. Sarah, this is my Mum, the reason for my existence."

Mrs. Evans grasped my hand and shook it warmly. "Please do come in, Sarah. How nice that a friend of Trevor's will be staying with us. He says that you're from the States, but with a name like Morgan, you must have Welsh blood."

"So I'm told. That's one reason I wanted to see Wales."

"Sarah's a writer," Trevor said. "She's here doing the book shop rounds with a talk show thrown in for good measure. That's how we met."

Mrs. Evans smiled, her eyes twinkling. "You probably couldn't help meeting my son. Ever since he moved to London, he's become very sociable. His outgoing side shows up every time I turn on the telly to see him on one show or another. Would you believe that he was the quietest of my two boys? When he was little, I never had to look far for him. He was either buried in a book or drawing instead of playing outdoors. Now it's hard to believe that this witty adult was that quiet, sober little boy."

Trevor gave her a hug and a brief peck on the cheek. "I still do have my quiet, sober moments, Mum. Sarah can vouch for the fact that I was being very quiet and well behaved on the train until Tom phoned me and she misinterpreted my end of the conversation."

I reddened. "I doubt that your mother wants to hear about that."

He shook a finger at me. "Don't think you can wiggle out of that so easily, Miss Morgan. It's too good a story to hide."

Mrs. Evans laughed. "Like any mother, I never turn down an opportunity to hear other people's impressions of my sons. Just so long as they're favorable."

I felt close to Trevor's Mum already and completely at home amid the stunning array of chests and bookcases of polished woods in her parlor. They

60

were complemented by cozy chairs and sofa in a blue chintz that matched the china visible in a hutch dominating the dining room beyond. It was clear that she was an accomplished decorator and collector of antiques handed down for generations.

"First thing tomorrow morning," she was saying, "I expect you to join us for breakfast, Sarah, and share the story about Trevor before making plans. There's so much to see and do in this part of Wales. Do you have any particular places in mind?"

"Actually, Mum, seeing the countryside isn't on her agenda this weekend, but I hope she'll come again for that reason." Trevor paused and took a deep breath. "She wants to look into the disappearances for another book. I knew we could help."

Mrs. Evans' smile faded. "I see. Does Enid know?"

"Not yet." Trevor turned to me. "One of the victims was Enid's sister."

I felt the blood drain from my face. "Oh, I'm terribly sorry. I had no idea there was a connection with your family. Will my being here bring up unhappy memories? I certainly don't want to hurt anyone's feelings."

"Not at all, Sarah," Mrs. Evans said. "On the contrary, I'm sure that Enid would welcome anything you can find. The authorities were at a loss to explain the disappearances, especially since none of the victims had any reason to run away or commit suicide and no bodies have been found. At the same time, they couldn't come up with evidence that murder was involved, and there are no suspects. But we can talk about it tomorrow. It's late and I know you want to see your cottage. Would you like a cup of tea and some Welsh cakes before you go?"

"I'll take a rain check on that, thank you. It's been a very long day."

"I understand perfectly." She located the keys in a cabinet drawer and handed them to Trevor. "Be sure to show Sarah where we keep the extra blankets."

"You may need them," he told me. "It can get very cold at night when the fog rolls in, even in June."

In the brief time we had spent with Mrs. Evans, the last vestiges of sun were sliding below the horizon. Reflected on high as a sheath of white against a starless sky, it marked the transition between twilight and night. Trevor picked up my overnight bag with one hand and took my elbow with the other to steer me along the slate walkway connecting his mother's home, Meredith's home, and the guest cottage at the far end. He nodded inland toward a thick hedge. "That hawthorn separates our property from our neighbor's pasture."

"How much land do you have?

"Altogether, including our three cottages and the driveway connecting them, we own about thirty acres." He pointed in the opposite direction. "If you look toward the water, you'll see the stone fence that marks the edge of our land. Beyond it is the Pembrokeshire Coastal Path."

" So near to my goal, and yet so far."

He paused to look down at me, his gaze steadfast. "I'm confident that fate brought you here to solve the mystery, Sarah. All you need is one useful clue. People come from all over the world to walk the path for miles alongside the sea. Surely someone along the way made an observation that will hand you the key."

"Confidence like yours is exactly what I need. Between your encouragement and Meredith's archives, I can't help thinking positively."

When we reached the guest cottage, Trevor set my bag on the doorstep. "Do you have time to spare a couple of minutes to drink in the view? It's still light enough for a preview of what's in store for you tomorrow."

"An orientation is definitely in order. That should help me firm my plans."

"Then be my guest in your brief introduction to this paradise for fishermen and nature lovers."

So saying, he led me to the fence and helped me over the stile. Moments later, we stood on a rocky promontory, buffeted by a wind that might have been sufficiently violent to hurl us over the edge were not the overlook guarded by a chain-link fence. Far below, the surf dashed against cliffs thickly populated with reclining seals. Judging by the chilly air, I knew that the water must feel icy to the brave souls wading in the surf, most of them bundled in heavy sweaters and parkas.

"I'm astounded that anyone's out there this late at night," I said. "Their feet must be frozen."

Trevor laughed. "Those are bound to be tourists determined to enjoy the long day, even if it means losing a couple of toes. Some of them come here thinking the Welsh beaches are fit for swimming, but the natives know better. As the story goes in St. Davids, where visitors often head for the beach, only a holy man could survive in the Irish Sea."

"Is St. Davids a resort?"

"No, it's more a tourist destination for people who admire early architecture. It's the smallest city in Great Britain, even though it's the size of a small village."

"Then why call it a city?"

"A huge cathedral was built there in honor of the Welsh patron saint," he said.

"And it still stands?"

"Yes, even though it's so ancient it could do with major repairs.

"It must be impressive."

"It is, especially because of the location and the ingenious way it was constructed so it can't be seen from the sea. Pilgrims from all across Europe have come there for centuries. They believed that three visits to St. Davids were equivalent to one to pilgrimage to Jerusalem. If you like, we'll drive down there to see the cathedral and ruins later this weekend. It's not far."

I was intrigued. "I've always been fascinated by old buildings and ruins. From what I've seen and heard so far, I'm beginning to think that I'd like to scrap my tour and spend the rest of the month in Wales. But of course that's not possible."

"Think of this weekend as an appetizer. We'll look at your schedule and block out as many days as we can for you to come back."

"You're very kind, Trevor, but you can't neglect your work for my sake."

He squeezed my elbow. "Sarah, the moment you accosted me on the train, your time became my time."

Unsure of what to say, I shivered. His presence was the cause, but he interpreted it otherwise. "Look here, we can't let you catch cold. You're not dressed properly for this climate, so we'll get you settled for the night, and tomorrow morning I'll bring over a warm sweater." So saying, he hugged me and rubbed my shoulder vigorously, as one might warm a child.

As we hurried back to the cottage, I saw that lamps within were already glowing, casting a friendly light across the garden. Trevor unlocked the door and handed me the keys. Leading the way, he pointed out various features in each room, from the location of light switches to the blanket chests. The cottage was every bit as cozy and attractive as his mother's home, its air permeated by the scent of fresh roses displayed in vases throughout and the aroma of linens dried outdoors in the sun.

"This is absolutely charming." Before reason took hold, I added, "I could live here forever."

He raised his eyebrows and grinned. "Is that a promise?"

I felt the blood rise to the roots of my hair. "Oh, I didn't mean…"

"Silly me. There I go misinterpreting a casual comment, just like a certain person we both know." The corners of his eyes crinkled in laughter and I could not help returning the smile.

"So we're even," I said.

"Maybe." His eyes bore into mine. "A slip of the lip often says more than measured remarks. Time will tell. In the meantime, we both can look forward to a weekend that I promised you will be strictly business. I'm obliged to keep that promise, Sarah, even though under any other circumstance I'd be sorely tempted to take you in my arms and kiss you goodnight." Overlooking my gasp, he added, "Enough said, this time around. Sleep well. I'll see you tomorrow."

    Before I could gather my wits, he was gone.

CHAPTER SEVEN

The First Victim

I awoke to the sound of laughter outside. Even though the bedside clock registered shortly after seven, sunlight streamed into every window of the cottage, as bright as mid-day. Scrambling out of bed to see where the voices originated, I remembered that I was only a few yards from the Pembrokeshire Path. A quick glance out the window confirmed that the voices were those of hikers enjoying the seascape and lure of the open road.

Eager to explore my surroundings, I retreated to the bathroom for a quick shower, but the mirror caught me off guard. Unwelcome traces of Raphael's handiwork cautioned that nothing short of a radical revision would erase his mistake. Just as I located a bottle of shampoo in my bag, a ringing telephone sent me scurrying toward the source. I found the instrument in the kitchen.

Lifting the receiver, I remembered Trevor's advice and said, "*Bore da*."

"And *bore da* to you, Sarah Morgan. You're a quick learner. Did I waken you?"

"No, not at all, Trevor. I was about to shower and banish the gook from my hair."

"An admirable decision. How long until the transformation is complete and I can pick you up for breakfast?"

"A half hour should be ample."

"Perfect. That's how long it will take for Enid, Meredith, and their two toddlers to join us at Mum's. Wear your oldest clothes. The twins are overly affectionate and sticky-fingered."

"You make it sound very homey. I can hardly wait."

"How shall I interpret that?"

"Any way you like." I smiled as I replaced the receiver in the cradle.

Exactly a half hour later, he knocked at the door. "You're very prompt," I said, marking how well his wholesome good looks fared in cords and a rugged sweater.

His large frame filled the doorway as he stepped across the threshold. "I aim to please, especially when a certain Sarah Morgan is involved. It's still chilly outside, so Mum sent you one of her warmest cardigans."

He held it steady while I slipped into its soft depths. "It's lovely. Is this what they call a fisherman's knit?"

"So it is. The style originated in Ireland, but it was adopted long ago as a standard Welsh craft, thanks to our huge sheep population. While you're here, we'll stop by one of the local knitting mills and pick up one of your very own."

"I'd love one. This is so warm and cozy."

He studied me for a moment. "It suits you perfectly, or perhaps I should say that you suit it. By the way, you look much better this morning than when I last saw you. Must be the hair."

"A little soap and water can do wonders," I said.

"And so can a hearty Welsh breakfast. Are you ready?"

"Absolutely." I smiled up at him and accepted the arm he offered.

We arrived moments ahead of Enid and Meredith, each clutching a rambunctious child with one hand, a battered teddy bear with the other. Once the boys were swathed in large bibs and settled at the table, Enid turned her attention to me. Like Mrs. Evans, she was the picture of robust health with rosy cheeks, naturally curly hair that thrived in a damp climate, and a demure mien enhanced by long, sweeping eyelashes.

"It's good to meet you, Sarah." She extended her hand and shook mine warmly. "Meredith explained why you're here. We're so very grateful. There must be a logical explanation for these disappearances."

"I may not be of much help, but the little I've read about the situation leaves a lot of empty holes."

"That's exactly how we feel. I know that your purpose is to write a book, not to solve a crime, but there's a chance you can uncover a clue that others have overlooked. At least we can get you started. After we eat, I'll tell you a little bit about Gwen, my sister, and later this morning you can go to Meredith's office. He'll give you access to the newspapers that carry accounts of the disappearances and the various police reports."

"I fell into a bonanza when I met Trevor," I said. "If it weren't for him, I'd still be wondering where and how to begin. It was simply a fluke that we ran into each other yesterday and that his brother turned out to be editor of the newspaper."

"That's not the half of it." Trevor, standing nearby, had overheard and was determined to seize the moment. While the adults gathered around the table, he regaled everyone with a blow by blow account of our meeting on the train and subsequent chase to the Roman baths, turning it into an event even more humorous than it had seemed to me in retrospect. His mother, brother, and sister-in-law laughed until tears rolled down their cheeks, and the twins, sensing Trevor's authority as family comedian, pounded the table and shouted, "Unka Twevah! Unka Twevah! Unka Twevah!"

The breakfast, a veritable feast, began with an enormous platter of fruit and local cheeses, followed by eggs, bacon and sausages, tomatoes, mushrooms sautéed in creamery butter, racks of "brown" toast, the Welsh descriptive for wheat, with assorted jams and jellies, and a choice of aromatic coffee or strong English tea. When we could eat no more, Trevor and Meredith insisted on cleaning up while their mother read to the twins, one snuggled on either side, and Enid and I settled on the comfortable sofa in the corner.

"Gwen is the happiest person I ever knew," Enid began. "She's eight years younger than I and extremely talented musically. She plays the piano beautifully, but her voice is exceptional and she won many singing trophies. She was studying to become a teacher and was home on summer holiday just before beginning her final year at the university. As if it weren't enough that her grades were outstanding, she had a contract to sing in the

Welsh Opera chorus during the upcoming season and an option to become a permanent member of the company. Her professional life couldn't have been better."

"Then that didn't figure into the picture," I said. "Was anyone jealous of her accomplishments?"

"Not that we know. But her career is only part of her life. Most importantly, she became engaged a few months earlier to a graduate engineer, a fine chap, who works for a computer company in Cardiff. He was devastated by her disappearance. After talking with him, we know that nothing had happened in their relationship to depress her. In fact, the very day she disappeared, I overheard her speaking with him on the telephone. The last words she said to him were, 'I love you, too, darling. See you next week.' There was absolutely no evidence that she had any problems whatsoever."

"It must be a nightmare for your family," I said.

"Yes, it is. Like Meredith and Trevor, Gwen and I lost our father many years ago and our mother was in poor health. If it hadn't been for Gwen's music teacher, she could not have gotten through those first weeks. He gave her tapes he had made of Gwen that she played all day long every single day for more than six months. She died of a heart attack, not knowing what happened to her daughter. We call it death from a broken heart."

"And the local police found no clues about Gwen's disappearance?"

"Nothing. She was in the habit of jogging on the coastal path, but so are lots of others. Even during the less crowded times of the day, hikers are visible in every direction. Somebody must have seen what happened or where she went, but nobody ever came forward. It's the same story for the other cases, eleven altogether."

"Could there have been an accident? Perhaps she was careless and got too close the edge?"

"The police ruled that out simply because the path never is close enough to the edge for someone to lose their balance. Of course you can leave the path to look at the beach and marine life below, but all the areas around the dangerous drop-offs are fenced and there are plenty of warning signs. You'd have to be very far off the trail to get into trouble."

"Yes, the lookout where Trevor took me last evening was fenced and I felt perfectly safe even though the wind was fierce."

Gwen folded her hands. "So there you are. I can't tell you anything more that might help. Perhaps when you examine the newspapers something will strike you that others have overlooked."

"That's all we can hope," I said.

Just then, Trevor emerged from the kitchen, rolling down his shirt sleeves, a sign that he and Meredith had dispatched the breakfast dishes. "Did you two have enough time together, Sarah?"

"It's a start," I said. "What Enid told me makes the disappearances all the more mysterious."

"Then we'll move along. Sarah and I will get a head start, Meredith, while you and Enid take the twins home. We'll meet you at your office."

I glanced up at him. "How will we get there?"

Trevor smiled. "We're not walking all the way to Haverfordwest, if that worries you. My car's in the shed behind the house. Between public transportation and taxis, getting around in London is a breeze and keeping a car there would be more trouble than it's worth. In this part of Wales, though, it's a necessity."

As we prepared to leave, Mrs. Evans said, "I know you have a lot to do, but I hope you plan to come back here for tea."

Trevor hugged her. "Don't worry, Mum, we wouldn't miss it. I want Sarah to experience the best of Wales. Your teas top the list."

Mrs. Evans beamed. "I'll try to not disappoint."

"If your teas begin to approach the breakfast we had, they must be fit for the Queen," I told her.

She placed her hand on my arm. "You're very kind. I'm so pleased that Trevor brought you and hope you'll stay with us often during your tour."

"Amen to that," Trevor said.

The drive to Haverfordwest in Trevor's unassuming Ford was less than direct, he explained, in order that I see the remains of several medieval fortresses visible from the roadway. "Don't think I'm bragging when I tell you that Wales has more castles and antiquities than any other country, but it's the truth," he said. "A world of history is encapsulated in this tiny country. We won't take time today to stop at any of the prehistoric sites along the way, but the next time you come I'll map out an itinerary that includes early burial chambers, standing stone circles that pre-date Stonehenge, castles, and ancient chapels built on druidic sites." He said that easily, as if my return were a foregone conclusion. The smile he tossed me activated those persistent shivers up my spine.

"If you weren't a TV cartoonist, you could make a fortune as a tour guide," I said.

He grinned. "It's easy to become enthusiastic about Wales. It's one of the most beautiful and mysterious places on earth and I'd like nothing better than to end my life right here where it began."

One glance out the window at the beckoning countryside and I understood.

At Fishguard, a village built on two levels and made famous by Dylan Thomas, he pulled into a car park near the bay. "What good luck," he said. "The water's calm enough for coracles."

"Coracles? Is that some kind of marine life?"

He grinned. "You're thinking about cockles, the creatures Molly Malone sold in song. The coracle is a one-man craft that's uniquely Welsh. I see several on the beach. I'd like you to take a close look at them before they go into the water."

We climbed from the car and hurried toward men unloading from their cars and trucks what looked to me like huge black bowls. Even as we watched, one set out across the sand looking for all the world like a turtle walking upright.

"Is that a coracle slung across his back?"

"It is."

"It doesn't appear to be heavy."

"No, they're made of split willow and are very light. For centuries, men walked miles carrying their coracles to the nearest river or stream to fish for salmon. That's the primary use, but when the weather allows, you'll see fishermen in the bay trying to land sewin, the native sea trout."

As we approached a knot of men, they grinned pointedly at Trevor, and one shouted, "Look who's here, mates."

Another cried, "It's Evans."

To a man, they swarmed about us, compelling Trevor to spend the next few minutes chatting about 'Torquaytoons' and what viewers could expect on upcoming episodes. At a break in the conversation, he introduced me and explained that I had never seen a coracle. That was the signal for them to speak at once, each eager to demonstrate his boat's unique features to a stranger from across the sea. One even insisted that I climb into his to test its comfort while he described how he constructed it from wood covered with unbleached calico and waterproofed it with linseed oil and pitch.

"They're made today just as they were a thousand years ago, and they do the job as well as anything fancy," he said.

Before returning to Trevor's car, we watched the fishermen trudge across the beach to the water's edge. One by one, they slipped into the coracles and began paddling through the shallows towards the deeper water.

"I feel as if I've been transported to a new world," I told Trevor, as we fastened our seat belts. "The countryside is so pristine, the air so fresh, and the people so friendly that it doesn't seem real."

He smiled. "It's very real, all right, the good kind of reality along with the bad. You're here to investigate the bad, but the good outweighs it by far."

"That's clear to see."

His broad smile confirmed that he understood and accepted my compliment.

By the time we reached the newspaper office, Meredith had freed a desk for me behind a carrel with a computer and printer alongside, and he had pulled up on the screen all the data I needed to go directly to the key issues containing reports of the mysterious disappearances.

"The staff is busy putting the Sunday edition to bed, so we won't disturb you," he said. "If you have any questions or need anything, don't hesitate to send Trevor after me. He knows his way around this place because he was our political cartoonist before he and Tom went to London."

I thanked him and settled down to the task of reading and printing everything pertaining to the disappearances, while Trevor made himself at home with his sketch pad an arm's length away. I worked for what seemed barely an hour, but the clock read well after noon when I glanced up and saw him beaming at me. Not saying a word, he held up his pad to reveal his latest creation, a toon with enough of my physical characteristics to make me blush.

"Sarah, meet Sally Sweet," he said. "She'll be arriving in Torquay about the time Gussie Glam fades into the sunset."

My stern expression could not conceal the smile in my voice. "I don't dare ask what kind of escapades you've planned for her."

"Let's just say that they'll be fairly true to life. After all, you did a yeoman's job setting the stage. How could I resist?"

"I trust that you'll keep my reputation intact."

"Have no fear. Sally will have all the traits of a lovable heroine, with a few eccentricities mixed in for fun."

"What kind of eccentricities?"

"Whatever her model reveals in my presence."

"Is that a threat?"

"Hardly. In fact, I promise that she has the potential to become one of our most popular and long lasting characters. But enough of your alter ego. How are you getting along?"

"With the records? Just fine, thanks. I've printed off everything pertaining to all the victims, enough to keep me busy conjecturing for several days. The main links between them are their age and the time of disappearance. All were last seen during the middle of the day. All of them sang in choirs, although I gather that's a foregone conclusion in Wales. Once I sort out the cases, I wonder how convenient it would be to speak with family members."

"Between Mum and Enid, they know most of the victims or their families. They should be able to help set up meetings. If you've done all you can here, we'll tell Meredith that we're leaving and will see him back at home for tea. Is that agreeable?"

"Whatever you say, Trevor. And please understand that I'm very grateful to you and Meredith for your help. I'm afraid that I've spoiled your day off and kept you from other plans."

"Not very likely. Having you here has turned

what might have been an ordinary, quiet weekend into an extraordinary one. As for my plans, it appears that you'll figure in quite a few of them from now on."

He helped me scoop up the sheaf of papers I had printed off and guided me toward Meredith's office. No matter how I struggled to exercise good judgment, I was beginning to want to figure in his plans, for a long time to come.

CHAPTER EIGHT

Probing the Unknown

We had traveled only a short distance from Haverfordwest when Trevor swung onto a narrow road and the car began a gradual climb. Above us, a mountain loomed darkly.

"We'll go home through Pembrokeshire National Park, one of the most beautiful places in Wales," he said. "A few homes are scattered here and there, most of them very old because today it's off limits to builders. Locals regard the park pretty much as a sacred area and make a great effort to keep it free of litter, as pristine as possible. I daresay it hasn't changed much since prehistoric times."

Even as he spoke, we passed the shell of a small castle. Further along, he pointed out several standing stone arrangements. "Notice the bluish cast," he said. "Those are the Preseli stones, like the ones used in the construction of Stonehenge. The main quarry's just a few minutes up the road."

"Stonehenge? But that's at least a hundred miles from here. Surely it would have been impossible for primitive men to move stones that size over the land."

"They were more resourceful than we can imagine. The ancient wise men understood astronomy quite well, considering that they lacked telescopes and instrumentation. They may not have mastered writing, but they were every bit as intelligent as modern man."

"They had to have ways we can't imagine to figure out how to construct Stonehenge."

"Without a doubt. Each stone was quarried to order. It's not clear how they communicated the exact size needed, but the method of transportation was logical. The stones were carried on rollers to the sea, then floated along the coast and up the Avon River to the Salisbury Plain. Then they were laid upon rollers once again and moved several miles to the present site."

"Why was that particular location chosen?"

"Scientists conclude that the key was its unrestricted view of the sky," he said. "Word of mouth must have played a major role. It was a long process over many generations and the best theory so far is that it was connected with religious rituals."

When I wondered aloud how primitive men figured out the best travel routes and developed the engineering skills necessary for such a project, Trevor explained that Stonehenge was not the only one. Dozens of sites were built throughout Great Britain, all similar in design. Stonehenge is the prime tourist draw today because most of the stones are still in place.

We had turned onto a rough track lined by a forest of pine on one side; on the other was a barren mountain, its jutting cliffs a haven for rock climbers. We had traveled about a mile when Trevor braked abruptly.

"Let's get out for a better view," he said.

As we picked our way along the rock-strewn path, I saw that the quarry extended beyond my vision. Sheer, jagged cliffs soared skyward; piles of rubble chipped by primitive tools lay far below in the gully. When Trevor accidentally kicked a rock over the side, it triggered a series of hollow echoes as it clattered into others at the bottom.

"This quarry's been worked down through the centuries, and still the source appears to be barely touched," he said.

"It's a beautiful site, and the pine aroma is exquisite," I said. "The peace is overwhelming."

"It must have struck somebody else that way in another age." He indicated a hillside hollow barely visible through the pines. "That cave looks for all the world like it might have been the home of an ancient resident."

"Or a modern day wild animal," I reminded him.

He laughed. "Maybe you're right. Wildcats and wild boars need shelter. Let's leave before an unwelcome creature fancies us for lunch."

Back on the narrow road, we wound through ever-thickening pine forests until we reached a lookout. He urged me to step out and survey the panoramic view. "This park is a favorite of campers and pony trekkers," he said. "They need to be well prepared, though, because the moors just beyond the forests are inhospitable. Even though we're only a few kilometers from civilization, it feels as if we've left the world behind."

The view was majestic from all sides, a range of hills surrounding valleys so deep their floors were hidden. "It's beautiful in one sense, but it's also a bit frightening. I'd hate to be here by myself."

His eyebrows flew up. "Scared, are you?"

"I'm thinking of those missing girls. You said that we're not far from civilization. Nevertheless, if someone abducted them and brought them to a place this desolate, nobody would know. There's nothing but woods, rugged hills, and moors for as far as we can see. I'm sure if I screamed with all my might nobody would come to my rescue."

He regarded me with an expression impossible to read. "Well, go on."

"Go on?"

"Go on and scream. Let's find out what kind of attention you attract."

"You're serious?"

"Absolutely."

"Then here goes." I took a deep breath and let out a scream that brought a smile to Trevor's face and his hands to his ears.

The echo doubled back several times, followed by utter quiet. Only the cry of a hawk circling above intruded the silence.

"You've proved your point."

"Which is…?"

"Nobody heard you," he said. "That proves this is an ideal hiding place, assuming that the girls were abducted. Trouble is, there are hiding places like this throughout Wales."

"From what I read, there was no evidence of abduction except for a purse dropped by one of the girls on the Pembrokeshire Path. It's been nearly a year since the first disappearance. How could anyone keep eleven girls hidden for that length of time? They certainly couldn't be maintained in a simple cave."

"Probably not. However, if they weren't abducted, didn't commit suicide, and didn't run away, they must have gone voluntarily, most likely with someone they knew."

"But with whom? And why? And why haven't they resurfaced, dead or alive?"

I caught a half smile. "You're the mystery writer, Sarah. Do you want to continue the pursuit?"

"By all means. I only wish I knew where to look next."

Trevor pulled out his mobile. "Let's try Enid."

Within two minutes, he had contacted her and jotted down the address and phone number of another victim's family. A second call later, we were on our way to meet the parents of Susan Jones, who disappeared several months after Gwen.

The Jones farm, located a few miles beyond the park's northernmost boundary, might have served as an artist's model, so neat and picturesque were the farmhouse and surrounding buildings. Sturdily constructed of thick, whitewashed stone, they encircled a lush farmyard bordered by hollyhocks. In the distance, flocks of sheep ranged contentedly within the hedgerows. Trevor parked in the farmyard, its surface paved in native stone to discourage dust. Alongside was a red tractor so shiny it might have arrived fresh from the factory that very day. The aroma of herbs filled the air and chattering magpies strutted beneath great oak trees.

Butterflies and bees flitted among the flowers lining the front walkway. The door opened before we could knock.

"I'd have known you anywhere, Evans. You're the image of your mother." The plump, pleasant woman grasped his hand, then turned to me. "And you must be Miss Morgan. I'm Ann Jones, Susan's mother. Please come in and make yourselves comfortable. You don't know how Gareth and I appreciate anything you can offer about Susan's disappearance. We're as much in the dark as we were the day she left."

As she spoke, a large, red-faced man appeared from the kitchen. His overalls gave evidence that he had interrupted his chores to acknowledge our arrival, and his damp fingers announced his effort to make himself presentable to guests.

Pointing to the upright piano where the photograph of a pretty young girl was displayed, he said, "That's our Susan." His gruff voice seemed on the verge of breaking.

The faces before me were hopeful. Fearing that they mistakenly believed I brought good news, I quickly explained that I could add nothing to what they already knew. I was merely seeking information about Susan's habits and interests not covered in the newspaper accounts.

I listened to their comments, delivered so rapidly that they seemed to tumble over one another, and mechanically entered the data on my laptop. Susan, like Gwen, attended college and had a lovely singing voice. Although her vocal coach had urged her to become a music teacher, she chose a business major. When I wondered aloud if music could be connected to the disappearances, both parents shook their heads. They pointed out that singing is a talent shared by the entire nation; the fact that the girls had been involved in choirs was inconsequential.

I turned to Trevor. "Do you agree that music can't be the link?"

He shrugged. "Perhaps it's no more important than the fact that all are nice young girls preparing for careers. Still, you're the researcher and I can tell by the look in your eyes that you don't want to jettison it as a connection."

I tossed him a grateful smile. "I'd like to keep all options open."

Even though Mr. and Mrs. Jones contributed some data about their daughter that the newspapers had overlooked, nothing striking stood out. Before saying our goodbyes, I closed my computer, hoping that I had acquired a future "aha!"

On the way home, Trevor pulled into the parking lot of a knitting mill. "They offer tours, but we'll save that for another day and head straight for the shop," he said. "You'll need a warm sweater of your own and the styles and quality here can't be beat."

There were so many beautiful sweaters on display, it was hard to choose, but at last I selected one almost exactly like his mother's. At the cash register, Trevor insisted on paying no matter how much I protested.

The clerk clucked her tongue at me even as she counted out his change. "Now you let your man have his way, young lady. Lucky you are to have such a gallant gentleman for a beau. He's a fine specimen, a real credit to Wales and not one that a lady should argue with in public."

Even without looking him in the eye, I sensed that Trevor was tickled by the woman's remarks and was filing them away in his mind for future use in "Torquaytoons." As we exited the shop, he said, "I hope her words were fair warning, lucky lady. Now that you have a gallant beau who's recognized by shop clerks, you can put away your credit card."

"You delight in embarrassing me, don't you?" We laughed like old, comfortable friends and he squeezed my elbow. Was it possible that we had known each other for little more than twenty-four hours?

By the time we reached her home, Trevor's Mum had prepared a tea table groaning with breads, pastries, cheeses, and seasonal fruits, none more delectable that the huge bowl of strawberries alongside another of clotted cream.

I gaped at the display. "It's a veritable meal."

Enid had arrived a few minutes earlier with the twins whose eyes, big as saucers, anticipated gustatory pleasure as their mother selected samples of everything for their plates. Mrs. Evans, serene and unflustered, presided at the steaming teapot.

"I was hoping you'd get back before the cheese scones and Welsh cakes cooled," she said. "They just came out of the oven."

Enid nodded in agreement. "They're a treat in themselves, but be sure to save room for Mum's chocolate and orange mousse. It's out of this world."

"The entire table is beyond belief," I said. "I've

never seen anything like it."

Trevor helped me into a chair and settled himself beside me. "Start with the basics, country ham on wheat bread, then work your way through the sweets. This should make up for our lack of lunch."

"This should hold me for the rest of the day and well into tomorrow."

"Don't be so sure." Mrs. Evans passed down a cup of aromatic tea. "Enormous appetites are the rule here. We blame it on the sea air."

True to her word, the feast she had prepared soon dwindled to stray crumbs on empty platters. Having savored his fill, Trevor stood, stretched, and lifted down each twin from his highchair perch. No sooner were the boys free than they scampered to the screen door and cast him wistful looks.

"Thwing! Thwing!"

"Beggars, both of you," he said, succumbing to their plea. "You have swings at home, but I've never known you to be content until you try out Grandmum's. Five minutes. No more. Sarah and I have places to go and things to see. Is it a deal?"

"Yeth, yeth, Unka Twevah," they cried in unison.

"Their own swings are tiny, but they love mine because it holds several adults and allows them to snuggle up together," Mrs. Evans explained as Enid and I helped her clear the table. "Whenever Trevor comes home, they make a ritual of coaxing him to sit there so they can listen to his stories about traveling to make-believe places."

"Sometimes I think that he uses the twins as

guinea pigs," Enid said. "If they react favorably, he knows the plot will work in his cartoons."

After making quick work of the dishes, the three of us joined Trevor and the twins in the garden, careful to mute our conversation so as not to intrude upon the magic underway. Trevor was transporting the twins through an imaginary country, sidestepping dastardly villains with every creak of the chains. Shrieking with feigned terror, they gazed into his face, mesmerized, awaiting the next move in their adventure. With the deft precision of an experienced television writer, Trevor contrived a timely climax, slowed their descent through the ether, and executed the landing in their Grandmum's garden.

"That should hold them until Meredith gets home," Enid said, as she commandeered a grubby fist and proffered another to Mrs. Evans. "Trevor, you and Sarah had better be on your way so Mr. Davis can get to choir rehearsal on time. I promised his wife you'd stop in directly after tea."

"If you think everything's under control, Sarah and I will leave," Trevor said. "Don't count on us for supper. We'll pick up something in Cardigan."

I shook my head in disbelief. "How can you possibly think about food after that incredible tea?"

Mrs. Evans smiled, as if withholding a great secret. "You'll surprise yourself once you become used to the Welsh customs."

Trevor took my arm and led me toward the door. In a voice meant for my ears only, he said, "And we'll make certain that doesn't take long."

The parents of Margaret Davis lived in Newport,

a short drive from the cottages. According to my notes, Margaret worked in a local gift shop during the day and was the alto soloist at the parish church. Again, the music connection dominated.

As we pulled away from the cottage, I was aware of hikers dotting the coastal pathway, each moving at his or her own pace, several jogging head first into the stiff breeze, others ambling along as if they had all the time in the world to reach their chosen destinations.

"How long is the Pembrokeshire Path?"

"Counting all the coves and inlets from Tenby to Cardigan, it runs for more than a hundred miles," Trevor said.

"If someone traveled from beginning to end, how long would it take?"

"A serious backpacker could cover the entire path in less than a week, but most hikers base themselves at one of the inns or a B&B along the route, branch out from there, and cover as much or as little ground as they like. Since the national park follows the coastline, the scenery is spectacular, no matter where you settle."

"This section is especially beautiful. How was your family so fortunate as to end up here?"

"We had the good luck to be born into a family that's lived along the coast for centuries. Our cottages go back to 1468, at least that's the date carved into one of the chimneys. We don't know if all three originally belonged to the Evans family, but they're similar in construction. Our ancestors acquired them and the surrounding land through inheritance. I've played around with the idea of a series about traveling back in time and meeting those early folks, but there would be some major problems."

"What kinds of problems?"

Trevor grinned. "Well, for starters, their personal hygiene might present a conflict to their modern counterparts. Baths and shampoos were saved for special events like holidays or marriages. Deodorants didn't exist and everyone had body fleas. Even Queen Elizabeth I, who enjoyed all the amenities of her day, kept King Charles spaniels under her skirts to lick the fleas from her legs."

I grimaced. "You've burst a bubble. In paintings, she looks so elegant in her finery."

"Oil paintings don't delve into the earthy aromas and crude aspects of the good old days. There's also the matter of size. Modern man is so much taller and sturdier, we'd loom over them like giants. If our ancestors met us by accident on a deserted road, all but the bravest would be terrified."

"Do you really think so?"

"I wouldn't be surprised, judging by the armor and clothing on display in our museums. As recently as the nineteenth century, men's shoes were closer in size to what you'd see today on a ten year old boy, and women's dresses and men's trousers would be better suited for modern children than adults. The average person living at that time was a good half-foot shorter and forty pounds thinner than his counterpart today, probably more."

"I had no idea there was such a difference."

"Most people don't, and I never thought about it myself until I read an article the minister of a Baptist church outside Cardigan wrote for Meredith's paper. He pointed out that the baptismal pool constructed at the end of the seventeenth century is no deeper than a small child's wading pool. He can't use it to baptize his members because he'd have to bend so low it would throw his back out of commission."

"I see. Since the actors playing historic characters in movies and on television are our contemporaries, the physical differences between modern and early man never becomes an issue in film."

"Exactly. Just one more reason why I've kept the project on a back burner. Maybe I'll dust it off in the future."

I pondered the matter as the car rounded several sharp curves in the road. "Since you'd be using cartoons instead of live actors, it would be possible to make that comparison. The size difference would contribute to the humor."

The gleam in Trevor's eye suggested that a light bulb had flicked on in his mind. "Sarah, you just set some creative juices flowing. Don't be surprised if you end up as 'Story line suggested by…' in the credits of my next project."

"You flatter me, but before I become involved in one of your projects, I'd better take a close look at 'Torquaytoons.'"

He grinned. "Don't trust me, eh?"

I blushed. "If you had asked that question yesterday in Bath, you know what the answer would have been."

He reached over and touched my hand. "What a

difference a day makes."

I was trying to formulate a proper reply when we rounded another bend and Trevor braked without warning. Had he not stretched out a protective arm, I would have struck the windshield.

"Sorry, Sarah. You all right?"

I nodded. Up ahead were several cars parked alongside the road, two of them with official beacons blinking. He pulled past them and cut the engine. After stepping onto the road to survey the situation, he came around to my window.

"Meredith's car pulled in right behind us, meaning something's afoot. He sends his reporters to cover the ordinary events, but if he smells news in capital letters, he's the first one at the scene."

"What is this place?"

"The village of Nevern is just ahead and St. Brynach's Church is down the lane to our right. I hear voices coming from that direction." He opened my door. "Come along. We'll see what's going on."

I hesitated. "Is it safe?"

"What can happen in a churchyard?"

CHAPTER NINE

Nevern and the Holy Rood

"This is the ideal setting for someone who likes mysteries," Trevor said, as we approached the stone chapel.

"Why so?"

"The Holy Rood."

I must have looked astounded because he grew serious, as if about to confirm an improbable truth.

"As the story goes, St. Helen, the wife of the Roman Emperor Constantine, brought pieces of the Holy Rood from Jerusalem to Wales during the fourth century and hid them nearby. They've never been found, but folks say that's only because nobody knows exactly where she buried them."

"That seems rather farfetched. Why would she bring them to such an isolated spot?"

"Maybe because she was born here and was coming back to her roots."

My mouth flew open. "Born here? That's something not covered in the history books."

"Perhaps not in your schools, but St. Helen and her deeds play an important role in Welsh oral history and as footnotes in our textbooks."

"Is there a record of how she traveled all that distance?"

"Not to my knowledge, but it's logical to assume that she came by both water and land. By the time Constantine ruled, the Romans were winding up their control of Britain. They arrived by water, just like Britain's other invaders."

I mulled that over. "Travel by boat is understandable, but it must have been tough going through the wilderness."

"Helen wasn't born in a wilderness. Roman legions had been stationed in Great Britain centuries earlier to build roads. When she came back with the relics, she would have followed roads she remembered from her childhood. Today the main highway across South Wales is known as Sarn Helen, meaning Helen's Causeway."

"Then maybe the story has merit. I was taught to believe that all legends have some element of truth."

Trevor took my elbow and steered me toward the end of the lane. "Probably more than are evident at first glance. Most legends can be traced back to verbal accounts of actual events by people unable to keep a written record."

"And subsequent generations are bound to add embellishments."

He nodded. "The farther you get from the original story, the more difficult it is to separate fact from imagination. Additions to a story can range from a few tweaks to so many lies that the truth is twisted beyond recognition."

Voices emanating from the cluster of men rose and fell in argument. Meredith, standing to one side, saw us coming and placed a warning finger to his lips. We waited next to him in silence while two men clad in jeans and woolen jackets vocally protested their expulsion from the premises. The four burly officers detaining them were accompanied by a gentleman wearing a three-piece suit and an air of authority.

Trevor looked a question at Meredith. "The Cross again?"

Meredith grinned in assent. He pointed to a cross that I judged to be two feet tall. It was carved into the rock face just beyond the church tower. "These men claim that the stone cross marks the presence of a secret cave behind the wall. Said they found an ancient manuscript confirming that the Holy Rood and other relics are hidden there."

Trevor raised his eyebrows. "And they planned to dig into the cave?"

"Seems so. Luckily, my friend from CADW got on their case and notified the police."

I asked Meredith to explain CADW. He described it as a government-run group whose role is to protect ancient buildings and sites throughout Wales. No excavations are allowed without their permission and the presence of a certified archaeologist.

"These guys obviously were trespassing and up to no good," he said, excusing himself to collect more details from Dr. Wilson."

As the police, one at each arm, began escorting the pair back to the main road, Trevor and I followed

Meredith toward the distinguished looking gentleman speaking on a mobile phone.

"They're taking them back to the jail right now," he was saying. "They'll be booked and held overnight, probably until the Monday court....Yes, I'll stay on at least until then...Nothing like landing a couple of cuckoos right here where the cuckoo myth began."

Trevor chuckled.

"What does he mean by that?" I asked.

"More myths for you, Sarah. According to tradition, the first cuckoo in Wales sang his song from St. Brynach's Cross, the marker you see over there in front of the church."

I moved closer to the marker, squinting, trying to read the carved letters. "I don't recognize the language. Is it Welsh?"

"No, the characters you see are a mixture of Latin and Ogham, an ancient Irish language. Similar markers are found at historic sites throughout Wales. Scholars didn't decipher them until last century."

"Who erected them?"

" Nobody knows, but they've guided travelers for as long as they've been mentioned in recorded history."

I shivered involuntarily. "I don't know why, but I feel as if ghosts surround us on all sides."

"Could be the yew trees," Meredith said.

"The bushes growing around the church?"

"Another mystery to whet your appetite. The largest is called a bleeding yew. Horticulturists say that the red liquid is sap, but old timers swear it's real blood. They're convinced that it bleeds for Christ on Calvary."

As Dr. Wilson completed his call, I chewed on the abundance of legends I'd become privy to within the last few hours. Just as I was beginning to sort them out in my mind, Meredith approached Dr. Wilson and beckoned us over for introductions. "John, I'd like you to meet my brother Trevor and his friend, Sarah Morgan, from the States."

Dr. Wilson brightened at the sight of Trevor. "I'd have known you right away, Evans, I've seen you so many times on the talk shows. If the B&B where I'm staying doesn't have a TV, it'll be the first Saturday evening I've missed 'Torquaytoons.'"

Trevor grinned. "Hearing that from a scholar is the nicest complement Tom and I could have. Many thanks."

"Thanks to you for giving us something to laugh about. It makes up for days like this when I'm called out to corral a couple of cowboys." He winked at me. "You see, Miss Morgan, I know a little bit about the States." He turned to Meredith. "Now how can I help you?"

Meredith pulled out his notepad. "Let's begin with the identity of the suspects."

"Glad to expose them to a proper journalist," Dr. Wilson said. "The thin one is Kenneth Grimes, who claims to be a minister, presently without a pulpit. The portly one is Raymond Baxter, a teacher of religion with a history of hopping from one private school to another. Both live near Mansfield in Nottinghamshire, quite a distance from here, but they're no strangers to Welsh sacred sites. We've been tracking them for the past three years."

"A couple of wily customers?"

"Wily and far ranging. Our sources uncovered proof that Grimes has financial backing for his various enterprises from as far away as South Africa and Australia. Just last year, he was ousted by the Turkish government for trying to round up a team of laborers in Ankara to join a trek to Mount Ararat and help him locate Noah's Ark. Claimed he had classified photographs of it with exact coordinates."

Meredith looked skeptical. "Where did he get them?"

Dr. Wilson smiled. "His story is that a satellite zoomed in on it. More likely, they originated in the dark recesses of his mind, along with other nutty ideas. He told one wire service reporter that the Ark is three stories high with a catwalk that runs almost its entire length and is broken in at least two pieces. Our spies say that he spent several weeks in Ankara trying to get the necessary permits. While he was waiting, he held daily press conferences trying to convince the officials and the public that locating the Ark would promote understanding and kinship among all religions."

"And they didn't buy it?" Trevor asked.

Dr. Wilson shook his head. "They sent him packing. Now he's back in Wales hoping to lick his wounds by finding the Cross. Give guys like this a pick and shovel and they'll commit more destruction in a few hours than erosion has done in a millennium."

"How do you keep them away permanently?" Trevor asked.

Dr. Wilson sighed. "Court orders haven't done the trick as yet. Short of fitting them out with computer chips that send an alarm whenever they approach historic sites, not much can be done. We rely on the public to notify the police. In this case, a couple of elderly ladies walking their dogs saw them unloading tools from their car and concluded that they were up to no good. By the time I was alerted and drove down here, they'd pried some stones from the wall and then refitted them loosely. Their plan, I believe, is to gradually widen the opening, maybe over a period of several days, and to keep their work concealed until it's large enough for Grimes to wiggle through into the cave. My guess is they've studied movies and TV shows about convicts digging their way out of prison."

"Do you actually think something historic is there waiting to be found?" I asked.

Dr. Wilson took a deep breath. "Perhaps. But one has to consider the options. Let's assume that there is something of value behind that wall. Would it be better to remove a physical item to a museum to be observed by the typical visitor for a few seconds, or to leave it here where belief in its presence adds a mystical aura to the land? Whether or not the cave contains something religious, historic, or both, the decision to remove it must be made by a body of experts from many disciplines, not by two pseudo historians."

Meredith nodded. "Their antics make a front page story, but not the kind Welsh readers like to see."

Dr. Wilson was about to say something when a door of the adjacent church slammed shut. Instinctively, we all turned in that direction just as a figure came into view.

"Oh, it's Phil Griffith, the choir director," Meredith said. As the newcomer neared, he greeted him with, "*Noswaith dda*, Phil."

"What did Meredith say?" I whispered to Trevor.

Trevor smiled. "Language lesson number two, Sarah. *Noswaith dda* is another way of saying 'good evening' in Welsh."

Phil Griffith moved quickly toward us, his brow wrinkled. "*Noswaith dda,* Meredith. What might this mean?"

"A bit of a flurry, but the authorities have everything in hand." After introducing us all around, Meredith briefly explained the situation to Phil.

"Oh, my." The newcomer clutched his chest. His voice was high and reedy, not unexpected in one whose vocation is singing. "The Holy Rood and the Holy Grail belong to Wales. Losing them would be every bit as dreadful as losing our musical heritage."

Dr. Wilson raised his eyebrows. "The Holy Grail? Where does it come in?"

"Why, it's at…" Phil Griffith ceased speaking so abruptly it seemed that invisible spirits might have clapped warning hands across his mouth."

Meredith covered for him, rather smoothly, I thought. "Another myth, Dr. Wilson. This one has been circulating around Cardiganshire for years. Probably no more to it than the rumors of the Virgin Mary buried in the Brecons and Joseph of Arimathaea in a grave near Cardiff."

Dr. Wilson frowned. "I've heard those tales, of course, but not one about the Holy Grail. Tell me what you know, Meredith."

"According to legend, it was hidden for nearly a thousand years in a recessed chamber under the high altar at Strata Florida."

Dr. Wilson nodded. "Ah, yes, the abbey where the Welsh nobility were buried. But I've never heard anyone connect it to the Holy Grail."

"That's probably because local folks call it the Nanteos Cup," Meredith said.

Dr. Wilson's eyes lit up. "My understanding is that the Nanteos Cup belonged originally to a magician, someone like Merlin. Pilgrims have sought it as a cure for centuries. You're telling me that people accept the Nanteos Cup and the Holy Grail as one and the same?"

Meredith nodded. "A vicar from Aberystwyth told me everything I know about it. It would have made a good story for my paper, but he warned me that it would draw the kind of people who could do great harm."

Dr. Wilson rubbed his hands together. "Please go on. I can't stand the suspense."

Seeing that we all were intrigued, Meredith obliged. "The vicar regularly visited members of his congregation and one day paid a call on a Miss Powell, an elderly parishioner who lived by herself in Nanteos mansion. Before he left, she told him she wanted to show him a valuable religious object that had been in her family for generations. She took him into a small room and showed him what appeared to be a portion of what once had been a wooden cup. When he saw that most of the sides were gone, and little more than the base and the bottom of the bowl remained, he suspected that small pieces have been chipped off as relics over the years. Miss Powell kept the cup in a glass case with a drawer in the bottom filled with letters. He glanced through a few and found that all were testaments to renewed health after drinking from the cup."

"A typical story about objects said to have healing qualities, "Dr. Wilson acknowledged. "But how did that particular cup become linked with the Holy Grail?"

Meredith glanced toward Phil, expecting him to respond. Nothing came forth, so he continued. "That part of the story goes back to Glastonbury. When Henry the Eighth ordered his men to burn down the abbey, seven monks escaped and made their way to Strata Florida. They regarded Wales as a safe haven because they were familiar with the tradition that Helen brought pieces of the Cross and the Holy Grail here in 325 A.D. They admired her determination to dig them up from the spot where the Emperor Hadrian had ordered them buried two hundred years earlier and carry them to a safe haven.

"Once they settled into Strata Florida and were shown the cup by those already living there, they worried that the King's army would ravage this monastery as well. So they delivered the cup to the trustworthy Powell family who lived in nearby Nanteos mansion, and that's where it has been kept to this day."

Dr. Wilson scratched his head. "Very interesting, Meredith. You newspaper people have access to stories that never come across my desk."

While the men talked, I noted that Phil fumbled nervously with his hands, alternately wringing them and picking at his cuticles. At length, he said, "Well, it's been a pleasure seeing you, but I must hurry along to my male chorus rehearsal in Cardigan."

"Sorry to keep you," Meredith said. "I thought you held all of your rehearsals here at St. Brynach's. At least that's where Gwen told us she came."

The veins in Phil's forehead twitched. "Dear, dear Gwen. Of course she would have told you that. I hold rehearsals for my children's and young women's choirs here because they are small groups and I can judge the voice quality and harmony with the piano better than I can with a heavy organ. My male chorus is much bigger and their voices so powerful that they require a large choir loft and the support of an organ. The church in Cardigan is the only one nearby able to accommodate a group of that size."

Trevor looked him directly in the eye. "Since your women's choir has lost so many members over the past months, do you have enough singers to keep it operating?"

Phil gulped. His eyes darted in one direction, then another, as if seeking an escape route. "We recruit new singers all the time. Naturally, I'm always on the lookout for outstanding ones. Right now we have several openings for sopranos." His eyes fell on me. "Do you sing?"

Before I could answer, Meredith cut in. "Indeed she does. Sarah has one of the loveliest soprano voices I've ever heard."

I stared at Meredith. Had he lost his mind? I was about to deny the talent he had attributed to me when I caught Trevor's warning nod. Instead of protesting, I smiled weakly.

Phil rubbed his hands in anticipation. "Good fortune continues to come my way. You must join us, Sarah. We meet here every Saturday at five. Come to our rehearsal next week, perhaps a few minutes early for a routine audition."

"She'd love to," Trevor said, smiling down at me and squeezing my arm at the same time to caution against making waves. "You won't be disappointed."

"Well then, that's decided. Now, if you folks will excuse me, I must be on my way." With that, Phil hurried away down the path toward the row of cars parked along the main road.

"And so must we," Trevor said, tossing Meredith a knowing look. "Sarah and I are late for an engagement. Nice meeting you, Dr. Wilson."

As soon as we were out of hearing range, I hissed, "Whatever possessed you and Meredith?"

"Suspicion."

"Suspicion? You mean…?"

Trevor nodded. "Meredith has thought for a long time that Phil Griffith is behind those disappearances, but without bodies and clues, nothing can be done. Even though the last thing I want to do is get you involved, the opportunity that fell into Meredith's lap just then is too good to pass up. Do I dare ask if you sing?"

"I have Welsh blood, don't I?"

His brow relaxed. "Then there's a chance he'll give himself away. If you're willing to help out, that is." His eyes pleaded, "And if you're free next Saturday."

"I'll have to check my schedule, but yes, I'm willing to help, provided I don't disappear along with the others."

"That won't happen, Sarah. We'll see to that." His voice was confident.

My concern eased. I had an entire week to prepare myself for the unknown.

CHAPTER TEN

Ghosts of Antiquity

There was barely time to interview the parents of Margaret Davis before her father left for choir rehearsal. Their responses were predictable and varied little from the material covered in the newspapers, but when I asked if they had any reason to suspect Phil Griffith, both stiffened. Mrs. Davis immediately put me in my place, reiterating her defense of Phil's concern and consolation during the days following Margaret's disappearance.

"There's absolutely no connection," she said. "Margaret was one of his favorite singers, a great loss for his choir. She was on her way home from the shop where she worked and was taking her usual shortcut along the Pembrokeshire Path when she disappeared. Nobody grieves more than Phil Griffith."

Mr. Davis stood abruptly, snatched his jacket and cap from the clothes tree near the door, and shook his finger at me. "I've sung with Phil for years and I have complete confidence in him both as a choir director and a human being. Now if you'll excuse me, I needs be on my way. I'm section head and in charge of warming up the basses."

Trevor bounded up from his chair. "Please don't

be angry, Mr. Davis. Sarah is a very competent researcher. She has to cover every possibility. There's nothing we want more than to learn what happened to Margaret and all the other girls. Our family is every bit as concerned as you are. Meredith's sister-in-law is also missing, you remember."

Mr. Davis's expression softened. "Forgive me. It hasn't been easy these past few months not knowing where Margaret is. She had no reason to run away. Quite the opposite. She and the neighbor lad were sweet on each other and planning to marry after they saved enough money. She was as happy as I've ever known her."

I joined them at the doorway. "We understand, Mr. Davis. Believe me, I'll do everything I can to make some sense out of this. Since there's been no trace of any of the missing girls, there's every reason to expect that they'll be found alive."

He sucked in a deep breath and opened the door. "Then do what you must."

By the time we took leave of Mrs. Davis and headed back to the main road, a chill wind was driving heavy clouds inland from the sea. Rain droplets splattered the windshield.

Trevor flicked on the wipers. "I'd planned to take you to St. Davids, but the weather isn't cooperating. I thought you'd appreciate the town's mystical qualities. They're especially powerful this time of year just as the evening fades into darkness."

"Now you've made me curious."

"Good." He shot me a meaningful look. "Then

investigating Phil Griffith isn't your only reason to come back. For now, we'll take a quick drive around Cardigan, have a bowl of hot soup at a nice little restaurant across from the castle, and head back to Mum's cottage. She has videos of all the 'Torquaytoons.' If you'd like to get started on them, a cold, damp evening is as good a time as any."

I smiled up at him. "I'd love that. Your sense of humor and the reaction of everyone who knows the show have me dying to see it."

"I hope you're not disappointed. I'd like to gain another fan, this one in particular."

I blushed and changed the subject. "What is there to see in Cardigan?"

"History, history, and more history. We'll enter the town by crossing the Teifi River on a stone bridge whose underpinnings date back to the Roman occupation. Beside the ruins of Cardigan Castle built by the Normans and the medieval town walls, you'll see a very elaborate Guildhall that rivals the finest of Europe."

"You make it sound positively irresistible to a history buff."

"It's a lovely town. That's why those of us who grew up here keep coming back. Cardigan's been an important seaport and shipbuilding center since the Middle Ages. Between shipping out fish, farm produce, slate, and folks headed for America, it was right behind Bristol, Liverpool and London in importance until last century."

"And today?"

"Today the large cargo ships are gone, but there are plenty of pleasure boats and jet skis. The local resorts cater to water skiers, and windsurfers, as well as hikers. Whether for good or bad, the tourist industry reigns, as it does most places in the U.K. Folks not interested in sports come here to revisit the past or to see where their ancestors originated. It doesn't hurt that most of our castles and historic houses have their fair share of ghosts. Everyone wants to get a glimpse of them, just so long as they don't show up in the middle of the night."

"That's easy to understand," I said. "Does the Cardigan Castle have ghosts?"

"Ghosts galore. There's Lady Helen Lethbridge, who died of loneliness and wanders the halls continually looking for someone to love, and George Davies who committed suicide there. Folks say that he's a poltergeist."

I was hooked. "Exactly how does George differ from an ordinary ghost?"

"I'm not an expert on the varieties of ghosts, mind you, but from what I've heard, George Davies is a very noisy and destructive haunt. He smashes glass, tosses heavy objects at visitors, and is generally disruptive. But then, he's probably no more troublesome than the present human occupant."

"What do you mean?"

"The Lord Mayor of Cardigan wants to renovate the castle and open it to tourists, but the old lady living there, the last of many generations of the same family to occupy it, refuses to leave, despite a writ of condemnation."

"What will become of her?"

Trevor chuckled. "We're dealing with two

women of strong wills because the Lord Mayor also happens to be a woman. She ordered the castle to be closed for repairs, and it was, but during the night, the old lady had a caravan lowered over the castle walls onto the grounds. She lives there still and won't budge."

"Caravan? The kind gypsies travel in?"

"There's that language barrier again. Caravan is the name we give to what you call a trailer."

I brightened. "A trailer? I see. That makes more sense. But if she's barricaded there, how does she get out of the castle grounds to shop for food?"

"Like all conspiracies, there's bound to be more to this one than meets the eye. I suspect that politics are involved and the old lady has supporters who oppose the Lord Mayor. Some of the residents want to keep the town as it was before the tourist invasion. They see their way of life disrupted when bus loads of travelers clog the streets, so they want the castle to remain sufficiently decayed to draw tourists, yet deter them from tramping through the building and grounds for fear of breaking a leg. When elections roll around, the truth may come out."

"I've been in Wales less than a day and already I've learned about more mysteries than I ever expected to find. Are there others?"

He laughed. "We haven't cracked the surface, Sarah. Another Cardigan Castle legend revolves around two tunnels leading from the north tower under the River Teifi. One goes a half mile southwest to St. Dogmaels Abbey. The other goes southeast about three miles to Cilgerran Castle where all kinds of legends abound, one involving the abduction of the lord's beautiful wife. So far as I know, nobody has excavated the tunnels. They're said to contain remains of the armies who've tried to besiege the castle for a thousand years. The rumor of a curse upon anyone disturbing the enemy bones has been enough to keep people away."

"No wonder. Does anyone know who built the tunnels?"

"This is the land of miners. Burrowing through rock is a native art that began ages ago, if we can judge by the Stonehenge bluestones. My grandparents told me that the Welsh underground is a honeycomb of tunnels. Some of them are abandoned coal mines of fairly recent origin. Others, far older, were dug during the Iron Age by people who lived in caves. The tunnels were their passageways from one mountain settlement to another. Still others were dug later on by Celtic pantheists."

"Who were they?"

"Rather like your Native Americans. They worshiped nature. In pre-Christian times, most outdoor places of worship resembled Stonehenge. Once the Romans arrived with a new set of beliefs, their gods became confused with the ancient Welsh gods in people's minds and evolved into the Celtic saints. Wales has hundreds of small Christian chapels, but if you investigated their history, you'd discover that most are built on the sites of Celtic places of worship that, in turn, were built above tunnels constructed during the Iron Age."

I studied his face with admiration. "You're a walking history book."

He smiled. "Blame it on our schools. Not only

did our teachers insist that we learn Welsh, but they also stuffed our heads full of Welsh history, some of which may be completely fictitious. Perhaps that's why the Welsh are regarded as great storytellers."

"No wonder your cartoon is such a success. You're a font of stories yourself."

His smile made my heart lurch. "And may you never grow tired of hearing them."

By the time Trevor located a parking space on Cardigan's narrow streets, the rain had subsided, allowing us to indulge in a brisk tour of the quaint shops along High Street and a glimpse of the Guildhall and Castle before hurrying into the Granary.

"This is one of my favorite restaurants," he said, guiding me to a corner table near the glowing fireplace. "Everything served is grown organically, from the vegetables to the grain of the bread flour."

Between the cozy atmosphere and the delectable aroma wafting from the kitchen, I understood perfectly why he was drawn here. I pored over the menu, unable to resist. "I thought I'd never be able to eat again after your Mum's delicious tea, but I'm succumbing. Maybe something light."

"I knew you could be tempted. May I recommend the establishment's superb potato leek soup, a loaf of bread hot from the oven, and a pot of herb tea?"

I laughed. "There's no defense against the Welsh cuisine."

"Surrender is guaranteed." He beckoned to the waitress and, after placing our order, he primed me for the evening ahead by embarking on a litany of behaviors typical of the Welsh and the 'Torquaytoon' characters they inspired.

By the time we finished eating, I was doubled up in laughter. Back at his Mum's cottage, he fed the first tape into the VCR and alerted his Mum to make herself comfortable in her favorite chair. While her knitting needles clicked furiously, creating jaunty caps for the twins, Trevor and I relaxed on the sofa.

Eight episodes later, the grandfather clock struck midnight. I flew back to reality with a start as I reached for a tissue to wipe tears of laughter from my eyes. "That was the most fun I've had in ages, but I've overstepped my welcome. I had no idea it was so late. Please forgive me for keeping you up, Mrs. Evans."

She tucked her knitting into the basket, a contented smile on her face. "No apology needed, Sarah," she said. "I love Trevor's cartoons and never pass up an opportunity to see them again and again. There's nothing like a good laugh to make all the cares of the world fade away. You've only just tapped the surface of the shows. When you've seen them all, Sarah, you'll understand how addictive they are and what a wonderful service Trevor and Tom are doing by bringing humor into the lives of thousands of people they don't even know."

She spoke as if she truly wanted me to understand and love her son's work as much as she did, and when I glanced up at Trevor and detected the same amused affection for humanity in his eyes, I had the absurd feeling that I had come home.

Even before we reached the door of my cottage, the gray mist that followed us back from Cardigan had turned to a steady rain. Umber clouds shielded the bright night sky unique to the summer solstice, emphasizing the gloom. Trevor propped the umbrella on the threshold while he unlocked the door and switched on the hall light.

"You'll be all right, then, Sarah?"

"Just fine, thank you. Between the people I've met today, the delicious meals we've had, laughing so hard from your cartoons that I'm weak, and the comfy eiderdown, I'll be a goner the minute my head hits the pillow. I can't remember a day crammed with so many adventures, some happy, others a bit scary."

His eyes crinkled into a smile. "It's been a day to remember. I'm glad you made some headway investigating the disappearances. On the other hand, I'm a bit apprehensive about next week."

I frowned. "Next week?"

He clucked his tongue. "How soon you forget. Phil Griffith expects you to perk up his soprano section. Look, Sarah, if you'd rather not…"

"Don't be silly. Of course I'll play his little game because I think that's exactly what it is."

His brow furrowed. "There's a lot more behind those disappearances than a game."

"Under ordinary conditions, I agree, but did you study his face? He had a wild, almost deranged look. I'm not convinced that he's capable of doing bodily harm, but his expression and reactions suggest that there's something curious going on in his brain, anything from a personality quirk to near insanity."

His jaw tightened. "Then that's settled. I won't let you put yourself in harm's way."

"You needn't be concerned. Remember, I planned to investigate the disappearances long before we met. Your suggestion that I come here and stay in your family's cottage simply hastened my involvement."

"Nevertheless, I do have reservations that we won't go into now because it's so late. We'll talk about it tomorrow."

I smiled up at him. "I doubt that you'll change my mind, no matter what you say. Don't you see, this could be the break that's needed."

He gripped my arm. "You have a very convincing way about you, but the mere fact that you sense something odd about Phil is all the more reason why I'm sticking fast."

"Stick close if you insist. I won't mind. At rehearsal next Saturday, I'll simply take note of everything he says and does. In the meantime, I'll sift through the material I collected today and study each case. There has to be a clue somewhere."

Trevor sighed. "It helps to think so. If I know Meredith, he's already contacted the police about your willingness to become involved. Even though Phil's been one of their prime suspects from the start, this is the first real attempt to trip him up, so they certainly will want to meet with you ahead of time to instruct you about what and what not to do and say. A lot of families have been touched by the disappearances, and since these cases are all fresh in everyone's mind, the authorities want to solve them quickly. In the meantime, maybe this will take your mind away from the monotony of book signings."

My hand flew to my face. "Oh, Trevor, I'd

completely forgotten. So much has happened in such a short time that I lost track of why I'm here."

"All the more reason why you need your rest, Luv. Tomorrow will be another busy day."

"It will?"

"Perhaps not so busy as today, but I thought it would be a good idea to start off by observing Phil at work."

"How is that possible?"

"His male choir, remember? They rehearsed this evening. Tomorrow morning they'll sing at church. After the sermon, there's a Gymanfa Ganu."

"A what?"

"That's Welsh for a hymn sing. It's always the highlight of the service because everyone can join in. Remember, Wales is a musical country. The natives aren't content merely listening to a concert. They insist on being part of it. That's why we have such enormous choirs. The incentive is to perform at the annual Eisteddfod."

"There's another word I don't understand."

"But you will very soon. For Welsh people throughout the world, it's our most important celebration."

"I'm ashamed that I never heard of it."

"The more's the pity, Luv," addressing me thusly for the second time within a few moments. As he continued, I wondered if it was merely a common native term, or a hint of something more personal. "It's a huge gathering of singers, poets, and writers. The tradition comes down from the early Celts who worshiped the beauty of nature and music. Most of the participants are from Wales, but many others come from throughout the world to perform and to listen.

"You see, the word *Eisteddfod* literally means 'to sit,' and that's exactly what everyone does. They sit quietly while poets recite their poems and soloists and choirs sing, all in the Welsh language. The winners receive prizes. Probably the most desired are the crown given for the greatest poem and the chair for the greatest piece of writing."

"A chair?"

"Yes, a chair beautifully carved by a master woodworker. It gives the winner all the prestige he would enjoy holding a university chair."

"You mean like a chair in literature or history?"

"That's right. This chair is given with the belief that the writer will continue to pen great works as he sits in the chair and receives inspiration from his muse."

"What a fascinating tradition."

"Maybe you'll be so inspired to learn more about Wales that you'll stay for the Eisteddfod next month." He paused, his eyes penetrating mine. "If for no other reason."

I tried to appear nonchalant. "You've taught me more today than I can absorb for the moment. I'd better take the Welsh traditions one at a time, starting with the music we'll hear tomorrow."

"You won't be disappointed. Welsh male choirs are admired the world around, and this one is regarded as the cream of the crop. If nothing else, you can compare how Phil conducts the men tomorrow with the way he handles the women's chorus next week. As you said, there has to be a clue somewhere. Maybe you'll see a difference in his approach, or in the presentation."

"I admit I don't know what I'm looking for, but I'm willing to take the plunge. And Trevor…"

"Yes?"

"If it weren't for you, I'd still be wandering around Cardiff wondering where to begin. I can never thank you enough for all you've done."

He grinned. "For nothing. Good night, now. Sleep tight."

I burst into laughter. "That sounds like something you might say to your nephews."

"Just practicing."

"For what?"

He winked, rather mischievously. "That's something we need to discuss another day."

He gave me a brief salute, did an about face, and disappeared into the heavy mist.

CHAPTER ELEVEN

Welsh Voices

I awoke the next morning to a chorus of warblers exalting in the willow trees. Their inspiration came from the sun rising in the cloudless sky and the fresh breezes that had banished yesterday's rain now sweeping off the sea. By the time I dressed, Trevor was knocking at the door and my greedy stomach was anticipating another sumptuous breakfast. His Mum did not disappoint us, although she cautioned everyone to save room for the Sunday dinner that would be served shortly after our return from the chapel.

Prior warned, we all worked off our breakfast during a brisk walk from the cottages to the Pathway. From a scenic overlook, we paused to watch the porpoises cavorting in the calm waters and the gray seals slipping off the slick rocks to join in the romp. The twins squealed with glee at the antics below. Their sharp eyes followed the aquatic creatures weaving in and out between the inflatable tubes occupied by teenagers drifting lazily in the harbor. As if by tacit agreement, the playful porpoises nosed the tubes back to the sand, executed a series of flips and dives, then zoomed off underwater to await the next round of the game. Within moments, the tubers launched themselves anew and paddled to a depth where they could float with abandon until their comic playmates popped up alongside and propelled them back to the beach.

"Those are bottlenose dolphins," Meredith told his sons. "Can you say 'bottlenose'?"

The twins rose to the challenge, dissolving into hopeless giggles when their efforts failed.

We were entertained so royally by the twins and the amphibian creatures that we lost track of the time until Trevor consulted his watch. "Sorry to run, but Sarah and I don't want to be late for chapel," he told the others.

Meredith raised his eyebrows. "Checking out our friend?" Without waiting for a response, he added, "Good idea."

"You'll be amazed by the male choir," Enid called after us. "Their voices are magnificent. We'd come along, too, but you see how it is." She made a face of mock hopelessness as the twins, chattering nonstop, tugged on Meredith's arms to plead a closer view of the dolphins.

"No need to explain," Trevor said, laughing. "The day will come when you'll be able to attend the Gymanfa Ganu without worrying that they'll crawl under the pews and scoot away."

The chapel was already filled with worshipers when we slipped in through a side door and climbed the steep stone steps to the balcony. The tier of wooden benches appeared to be packed solid, but friendly smiles and beckoning forefingers urged us into the space that miraculously appeared at the end of the front bench when the occupants slid closer one another to accommodate two more.

Honoring the solemnity of our surroundings, they did not address us aloud, but their facial expressions and surreptitious nudges confirmed that they recognized Trevor. Gracious to a fault, they seemed drawn to him as a fellow countryman, not for his celebrity.

The brief sermon by a jolly preacher who orated in both English and Welsh was a mere introduction to the major event of the service. Once his message advocating peace and love of one's fellow man was delivered and acknowledged by the crowd, he acceded to the male choir massed in the great stall spanning the rear of the chancel.

Momentarily, Phil walked to the podium, signaled to the organist, and delivered the downbeat.

At the first thundering chord executed by more than a hundred voices, the congregation shifted as one to the edge of their seats. The sound ricocheted around the sanctuary. At times the basses were as profound as cannons on a battlefield; at others, the tenors sat atop notes so high and ethereal their voices might have belonged to cherubs. There was no escaping the beat that pulsated through my body, and though I knew no Welsh, I understood the text's message, so distinctly did the singers convey the themes of faith, fortitude, and willing sacrifice for the betterment of mankind.

Between selections, I turned to Trevor and whispered, "They're beyond belief."

He grinned. "If a Welshman has no other talent, he can sing."

And then there are Welshmen with multiple talents, I thought, as I returned his smile and felt his arm come around my shoulder, ostensibly as a prop. There was no point in trying to wriggle away; my prim and proper self had little chance of prevailing so long as my knees turned to putty each time our eyes met.

The musical portion of the service, the concert followed by the entire congregation joining in for the Gymnfa Ganu, lasted for better than two hours. When the entire chapel burst into glorious song, I quickly observed that everyone around us had a voice worthy of a recording contract, none surpassing Trevor's baritone. At the close, I was exhilarated, not weary. As the audience obeyed Phil's hand signal to rise, the organist began playing a melody I recognized.

Trevor leaned over to whisper in my ear. "This is '*Cwm Rhondda*,' usually the closing anthem. You probably know it as 'Guide me, O Thou great Jehovah.' Feel free to sing along in English."

As the music ended with a triumphant arpeggio from the organ, I scolded, "You should be in that choir. Your voice is better than any I've heard today, and they're all fabulous."

He laughed. "Your compliment is greatly appreciated, Sarah, but my ability is only average compared with Welsh choir veterans. Maybe someday when I've settled down here and have time on my hands, singing would be a pleasant hobby. In the meantime, there are other ways to make beautiful music." He gave me a quick hug, then shook hands with several people nearby who were trying to capture his attention.

"It's good to meet you at last, Evans," one man said. "My wife and I follow 'Torquaytoons' religiously."

Trevor laughed. "Not as religiously as you attend church, I hope."

Folks standing nearby who overheard laughed heartily and several pressed forward to speak, some old friends, others strangers drawn because they recognized Trevor from the telly. To each in turn he was kind and thoughtful, thanking them for stopping to speak and for doing their part in maintaining the beauty and friendliness of Pembrokeshire as he remembered it from childhood. His arm firmly across my shoulder, he introduced me to all as his friend from the States, emphasizing that he hoped to convince me to settle in Wales. I sensed that most of the people were curious about our relationship, but all were too reserved to press for more details. By the time we reached the parking lot, I had the delicious feeling that I was becoming part of the landscape, a wonderful option considering the beauty visible in every direction and the man at my side.

The lofty music was still pulsating through my veins when his words brought me back to earth. "Did you pick up any clues?"

"Clues? I'm sorry, but no. Nothing struck me except his great love for the music and the power of the human voice."

Trevor sighed. "Then he doesn't seem a likely villain?"

"It's too early to cross him off the list. Where music is concerned, he seems to be totally honest, but there could be a dark side he doesn't display on the podium."

"So you're still game to delve further?"

I smiled up at him. "Absolutely. Next week I join his choir. Meanwhile, I'll have to practice my scales."

"If you need a sound-proof room, you're welcome to use the one in our studio."

"I may take you up on that. When I get back to London, I'll check in with Elspeth to learn my schedule for the next week. Between book signings there should be time…if I knew how to find your studio."

"You don't think I'd let you wander the city streets alone, do you? I'll pick you up and deliver you there myself. Besides, I can't wait to introduce you to Tom."

"To assess the new character you propose adding to the series?"

He laughed heartily. "That, too. No, my intentions are purely selfish. I want you to meet my partner so you can understand a little better what makes me tick. He and his wife have a flat near Hempstead Heath. It gives them a view of some of the best nature found in London proper, although nothing like they had in Wales." He paused. "I hope you like them. I know they'll take to you as much as my family does."

"I'm sure I'll like them. Anyone behind the humor in 'Torquaytoons' is bound to be fun to know."

His eyebrows arched. "If I read between the lines, I take it to mean that you regard me as fun to know. Is that all?"

I stared at him, trying to weigh my words with no success. "To be truthful, I have to answer yes and no."

"Yes and no? Your mind's in a pretty muddle."

"Blame yourself."

I detected a grin. "Maybe it's my fault. This is classified as a business weekend, so I caught you off guard. Suppose we regroup and approach the next few weeks in a different mode. Would that help?"

I nodded.

He glanced at me sideways. "From my vantage point, that mode will be what my grandparents used to call 'courting.' Somehow the contemporary jargon doesn't do justice to my intentions." He reached for my hand. "Am I making myself clear."

Again, I nodded, swallowing hard.

"Good. Then I gather you have no objections if I pursue my quest on a level playing field."

I shook my head.

He looked a question. "No objections?"

"None," I said in a very small voice I scarcely recognized.

He beamed, and our eyes locked for one long, deeply personal moment. Then he changed the subject abruptly. His observation about the crowded chapel would have been mundane coming from any other source. Instead, the warm timbre of his voice and his magical gift of wit lifted my heart to heights I never dreamed possible.

Later in the afternoon, following the sumptuous family dinner, Meredith drove us to Carmarthen where we boarded a local train. At Swansea, we transferred to the high speed train and for the next two hours I feasted upon Trevor's stories of life in Wales and the idiosyncrasies of its people. So many things went through my mind as I sat, spellbound, next to the man who two days earlier I had mistaken for a murderer. By the time our train reached Paddington Station, I had trouble refocusing on the true reason for being in London.

He escorted me to the door of my flat. "Will you be all right, Sarah?"

"Just fine, Trevor. I've had a lovely two days with you and your family and maybe the beginning of another book."

"The pleasure was all mine, even though you mistook me for a murderer out to do someone in." He squeezed my arm. "I'll call you later, Luv."

Once my emotions were checked, I dialed Elspeth to confirm my schedule for the week.

She must have been clutching her phone awaiting my call because she answered on the first ring. "Sarah, Tara, tell me about your weekend. Is he as spectacular in person as he is on the telly?"

I laughed out loud. "Elspeth, I have no intention of dishing any dirt."

There was silence on the other end.

Quickly, I justified my response. "Besides, there's none to dish. Yes, he's very good looking and a gentleman from every angle. But so is his brother."

"He has a brother?"

"And a mother, and a sister-in-law, and two darling nephews."

"How did you spend your time?"

"We talked, ate, visited some historic sites, and heard some beautiful music."

"And...?"

"And that's about it."

"Oh." Her disappointment reverberated through the phone. "Will you see him again?"

"Actually, yes. He invited me back for next weekend."

Elspeth released the deep breath she had been holding. "Well, now, there may be a fascinating plot afoot after all."

"That's true, if you mean the Pembroke Path disappearances. There's something you should know."

"Yes?"

"Trevor's brother is a newspaper editor. He gave me access to information about the missing girls and the family made arrangement for me to interview several of their parents."

Elspeth squealed with delight. "What a book that would be. Can I assume that you've uncovered more details?"

"Enough to be encouraging. Trevor and Meredith, his brother, both think a book on the topic could be of interest."

"Of interest? That's putting it mildly. The prospect is almost as good as that of a romance between you and Trevor Evans."

"Be sensible, Elspeth. You're jumping to conclusions that aren't logical under the circumstances. I've known Trevor all of two days. Judging by the schedule you've arranged for me, there'll be precious little time to develop a relationship before I go home."

Elspeth's chuckle was sly. "I doubt that I'll have

to alter your schedule to suit his. If the match is as ideal as I suspect, he'll alter his to fit yours. Now, let's make certain you have this week sorted out, starting with the signing in Manchester tomorrow."

I made notes as she guided me through train timetables, the names of contact people at each book store, and places of interest in the event I had a few hours to play tourist in the designated towns. Once we plotted out the rest of the week, it seemed there would be little opportunity to think about Trevor, much less see him. Subdued, I rang off, feeling a bit down. And then my cell phone rang.

"Trevor?"

"Of course. What are you doing? I hope I'm not keeping you up."

I giggled. "Suppose I'd been asleep. Would you want me to tell a white lie."

He was quiet for a moment. "Truthfully, did I waken you?"

"No, you're exonerated. As a matter of fact, I've been mapping out this week and trying to get the schedule Elspeth has arranged into my head. It looks busy."

"Not too busy for you to visit our studio, I hope."

"Oh Trevor, I'd love to see it, you know that, but there doesn't seem to be a break."

"Read it off to me, Sarah. We'll work out something."

And we did. My Wednesday signing, an early afternoon affair, was in nearby Reading on the Paddington line, a brief half-hour ride from London. Trevor would pick me up at the bookstore after the event and the rest of the day would be ours.

"I can hardly wait, Trevor. Now that you've introduced me to 'Torquaytoons,' I'm dying to see where they originate."

"Have you no curiosity about spending time with the person who brings them to life?"

Laughing, I said, "Yes, I'm looking forward to meeting Tom Rhys."

He chuckled. "Be that as it may, I couldn't get to sleep without calling to wish you 'goodnight.' After two days of blissful companionship under the guise of business, are you trying to sweep me under the rug and throw propriety to the wind? Remember, my partner is a married man. I, on the other hand, am extremely eligible."

Behind his laughter, I heard a heartfelt plea that demanded the truth. I responded with all the sincerity I could muster without embarrassing myself by confessing exactly how I felt about him. "You know I'm joking, Trevor. I had a wonderful time with you and your family, especially with you. I'm afraid that the next two days will pass twice as slowly as the last two."

His voice came across the ether deep and low, twisting my stomach into knots. "Words like that can give a man all the courage he needs to survive." A pause. "Good night, Luv." His voice was so penetrating that we might have been sitting side by side, arms entwined.

Once again, my stomach lurched as I whispered, "Good night, Trevor."

CHAPTER TWELVE

Torquaytoons Unmasked

  Outside of nearly missing my train to Manchester because I failed to note that it departed from Euston Station, not Paddington, the book signing tour began faultlessly. Each store I visited featured my book in the window to lure pedestrians into the shop. Once they were inside, appealing displays invited them to snap up a copy. The community relations managers had done such a bang-up job publicizing my appearance in the local media that reporters, several with a photographer in tow, awaited my arrival. After answering their prepared questions and several random ones, I took my place at the table provided and turned my attention to the waiting queue of customers.
  At an adjacent counter, a store employee collected the cash payments and swiped credit cards to verify the book purchases. Only then were the bearers admitted into the sacred vale of author and admirers. So many copies were presented for signing that I would have sagged from boredom had not the personal dedication requested by each customer provided intriguing variances.
  By Wednesday, I had mastered the two signings

in Manchester and one each in Norwich and Ipswich, so the Reading bookstore appearance promised to be routine. It was not until the scuffle at the doorway grew out of normal proportions that I paused from the task at hand and glanced in that direction.

Photographers stood on counters above the crush of women waving hands, books, even teddy bears snatched from toddlers. All were endeavoring to capture the attention of someone entering the store. Magically, the mob parted before my eyes to allow the newcomer passage. He strode directly toward my table, pausing only long enough to select a book from the display and pay the clerk. The next thing I knew, he was thrusting it before me for an autograph.

"How...how...?" I began.

Trevor tossed me a mischievous smile. "How do you do, Miss Morgan. What a surprise to see you again."

I blinked. "Surprise?"

"Yes, you recall that we met backstage in Bristol. The name's Trevor Evans." A surreptitious wink signaled me to play dumb.

"Of course, Mr. Evans. It's a pleasure." Without looking around, I grasped the situation. The eyes and ears of every woman in the store were riveted on Trevor and the photographers and reporters were jotting down reactions and remarks as fast as they flew. If I made the wrong move, the tabloids could have a field day.

"You started to ask how the dedication should read. I'd like it to say 'To Trevor's Mum.' My Mum loves mystery stories. She'll be thrilled to know that I actually met the author."

"It's my honor."

He bent closer as I wrote the dedication and tried to maintain my composure. "My Mum also loves love stories. Modern love stories. About people she knows."

"She sounds like quite a romantic," I said, not daring to lock eyes with him.

"No more so than her sons."

Elspeth was right. Trevor was one of the most desirable men in Great Britain. The crush of women throughout the bookstore trying to catch a glimpse of him was ample proof of that. And he was here because he wanted to see me, nobody else.

I shut the book and handed it back to him. "Here you are, Mr. Evans. I hope your Mum enjoys this mystery."

"I know she will. Thank you very much, Miss Morgan. Perhaps we'll meet again." His voice dropped to a whisper. "May I suggest you drop by the psychology section when you finish?"

I struggled to suppress a laugh as he moved away amid a swarm of reporters asking why he bought my book. As the next reader approached my table, I heard Trevor say that it came to his attention when we both were guests on Sophia Rydal's show to be aired during the week. Whatever else he said was swallowed up in the noise generated by customers and journalists hungry for a story.

Several hours passed. After signing a book for the very last lady in line, I thanked the manager, then slipped away in search of Trevor. I found him sprawled in an easy chair perusing a book exactly as promised in a secluded corner of the psychology section. The prying reporters were gone. He looked up and grinned. "I'm searching for advice on maintaining anonymity in a celebrity-crazed world."

"Your popularity is mind-boggling, but for good reason. The public adores your cartoons and you by default because they've seen you on talk shows and connect you with 'Torquaytoons.' Consider their fervor as flattery."

"You put a cheerful spin on it, and you're right. Pursuit by the press is my reward for accepting invitations and sticking my face into the camera. Now that your beautiful face and book have been introduced to the world, it won't be long before someone puts two and two together. Do you mind terribly?"

"What are you talking about?"

He rose and took my arm, a serious expression on his face. "I mean, Luv, that you probably will be subjected to front page scrutiny. Especially when we're seen together. I can laugh at tabloid gossip, but I don't want you hoisted onto a platter and picked over."

"To answer your question, I don't object to being associated with you and I doubt that anyone would waste time gossiping about me. If asked, we'll tell the truth: we're acquaintances with a mutual interest in Wales."

A smile broke across his face. "Sweet and succinct." His voice lowered to a whisper. "But then you always are. What say we head out to the sidewalk and hail a cab?"

"We're going to your studio?"

"Indirectly. There are a couple of places I'd like you to see on the way."

An hour later, the cabbie dropped us off at Buckingham Palace where we melted into the mob of tourists from around the world, few of whom had ever viewed 'Torquaytoons.' Our privacy was assured. Along with the others, we looked in vain for the Queen and admired the Royal Guards in their bearskin hats. Trevor was simply another face in the crowd, not a celebrity to be sought out by reporters. But the inevitable was bound to happen. My spirits sank when a woman's voice, coming from a knot of tourists, shouted his name.

"Must be one of your fans."

He waved back at her, nudging me at the same time. "Not necessarily. Do you see who that is?"

"Oh, my goodness, it's Betty. And Dawn." Mother and daughter rushed forward, all smiles, sidestepping the stream of gawkers milling about the palace gates. "Imagine running into you two here."

Betty laughed. "It must be destiny. Dawn and I had such a wonderful time at the television station that I was planning to give both of you a call. We'd like to take you up on your offer to show us around your studio, Trevor, if you have time while we're in London."

Trevor nodded affably, although I caught a slight hesitation in his reply and wondered if it signified disappointment that our afternoon together had taken an unwanted direction. "Actually, you're in luck, provided you don't have plans for the rest of the afternoon. Sarah and I were taking a detour there. You and Dawn are welcome to come along."

"We don't want to interfere with your plans, but it certainly would be a treat." Betty looked a question at Dawn. "What do you say?"

"That'd be cool, soon as I take a couple more pictures."

That accomplished, we all strolled together down the Mall to St. James Park, pausing to contemplate the waterfowl strutting alongside the lake and splashing in the water. Dawn aimed her camera to capture the ambiance and snap close-ups of the some of the more aggressive birds trying to cajole treats from folks munching on snacks.

"The silence is surprising, considering that we're in the heart of a great city," I said.

"London's a city of parks," Trevor said. "No matter how harried you are and how heavy the traffic, it's soothing to spend a few minutes in one every day. Some people jog, some lie in the grass to soak up sun, some sit on a bench and feed the wildlife, while others simply enjoy the flowers."

"They're beautiful, and they're everywhere," Betty said. "Having a green thumb must come naturally to the English."

"And the Welsh," I said. "Trevor took me past some lovely gardens in Wales, including his mother's. She raises roses the size of dinner plates."

Dawn stood arms akimbo, rolling her eyes. "C'mon, Mom. Trevor's waiting to take us to his studio. You're not going to gab all afternoon, are you?"

Trevor raised his eyebrows and quelled a smile on his lips.

The studio was within easy walking distance of the park, several blocks off Piccadilly Square, in a generic office building that I later learned was home base for a number of film and television producers and agents. The security guard greeted Trevor warmly and participated in what I gathered was routine banter between the two as he checked the passports and other identification Betty, Dawn, and I had to offer.

"Looks like you have the start of a lovely harem, Evans," he said, tossing us each an overt wink as we signed his guest book. "The tabloids will be making a beeline to the door once this gets out."

Trevor laughed. "Remember that keeping them at bay is part of your job description."

"And one I enjoy, what with all the bribes that come my way. Some of the reporters have no shame." He clucked his tongue and patted his imposing belly. "All the better to insure that I eat well. They're always bringing me goodies from the local shops. But my lips are sealed."

"You wear your badge like a gentleman," Trevor said. "Charles and Camilla should have such a loyal subject."

"My pleasure," the guard said, rising to admit us to the hallway beyond containing a bank of elevators.

"Thanks, Fred, but we'll take my usual route," Trevor said.

Fred shrugged. "I thought the ladies would like to get there in style. Guess you can't teach old dogs…"

"New tricks," Trevor filled in. "You're right. Besides, the studio's only one floor up. We can climb the stairs about as fast as the lift can get there, especially on those occasions when it's not working." He turned to me. "It's been balky more than once. Once is one time too many to get caught inside when it decides to act up.

That's why I take the stairs."

"And it's good exercise, besides," Betty said, as we reached the next landing.

Trevor smiled. "Spoken like a true athlete. Just down the hall a few doors and we're there."

Dawn was the first to enter the studio, scurrying ahead to soak up everything at a single glance.

Even before I passed through the doorway, I heard her ecstatic squeal. "Look at these, Mom. Did you ever so anything so cute?"

Trevor ushered Betty into his office in with a flourish before tossing me a wink. "Dawn is gushing over the puppets, and I dare say Tom also has caught her attention."

The sound of a male voice mingling with Dawn's confirmed that Trevor's partner was already contending with the impressionable teen.

"Puppets? I see what you mean," I said, as we passed through the entryway into a large space accommodating several easels, shelves of art materials, a bank of computers, and photographic equipment. It was populated by dozens of figures that might have been plucked from the throngs of people we had passed on Piccadilly, but these life-sized characters straight out of someone's lively imagination were lodged on bookcase shelves, suspended by twine from the overhead light fixtures, and casually reclining on windowsills, the backs of chairs, and even perched atop the desk of the bespectacled woman who was speaking on the telephone and simultaneously managing her secretarial duties with practiced serenity amid the chaos.

Dawn had reached the far side of the room and was nodding vigorously as the pleasant looking man by her side explained the role of the cuddly figure cradled in her arms.

I whispered to Trevor, "Are we allowed to touch the puppets? They look very authentic and very valuable."

"Touch all you wish. The fact that Dawn was drawn to old Ebeneezer Geezer, the local eccentric, the minute she walked in is confirmation of his appeal to the television audience in general. Like all the puppets, he's a three-dimensional pattern of the original drawings. A toy manufacturer made them for us after the series became popular, and smaller versions are sold in better stores. I suppose he's valuable, but I doubt that would deter anyone from hugging him if they were so inclined."

Concern spread across Betty's face. "Please speak up if you think that Dawn could damage the puppet."

The secretary, overhearing, looked up from her phone conversation. "Don't you fret, ma'am. My son welcomes fans. They're what keep this office going."

"Annie's absolutely right; we're here because of the viewers," Trevor said, as he took my arm and explained, "Annie Rhys, Tom's Mum, is worthy of first prize for office manager of the year. If she hadn't volunteered to come to London and do all the real work that goes on around here, we never would have landed our first contract. Now she's indispensable."

Acknowledging us with a warm smile, Annie completed her telephone conversation in a voice gilded with a lilt that stamped her Welsh heritage. Once the receiver was back in its cradle, she turned her attention to us and offered her hand as Trevor presented Betty and me.

Her smile was warm and motherly as she said, "Trevor hasn't stopped talking about you since Monday, Sarah, so I've been dying to meet you. I hoped he'd bring you around. but I was afraid that you'd be too busy to take a break from your book tour."

"The signings have approached controlled chaos, if that's what you mean. Coming here is a treat. I've never been behind the scenes of a television show."

Trevor grinned. "How quickly you forget."

"I mean *really* behind the scene. Believe me, Trevor, I haven't forgotten that talk show, especially the last few minutes when Clyde Dale and his combo were making that racket and we had to keep dancing until the show went off the air."

"Ah, those stolen moments with you in my arms..."

Annie tossed him a look of feigned disapproval. "Trevor, what have you been up to behind my back?"

"It was all in fun, a fantastic show," Betty said. "Trevor and Sarah were wonderful. During the closing act, they looked like they were having the time of their lives. And afterward, Trevor introduced me to that marvelous actress, Lucy Cox. I've been a fan of hers for years. The hostess, Sophia Rydal, was so good looking and clever, and Dawn was crazy about Clyde Dale. Seeing that show has been the highlight of our trip so far. It's a shame you missed it."

"No worry about that," Trevor said. "I believe it's scheduled to air on Friday. Check the television listings, Annie. You'll see us as we never wanted to be seen. Sarah especially. Be sure to notice her attractive hair style."

"Please don't," I murmured, as his arm came across my shoulder and gave me a warm squeeze.

"You looked cool on the TV show." Dawn, still clutching Ebeneezer and approaching us with Tom in tow, had overheard. "The way your hair was fixed is exactly how I'd like to do mine."

"Not if I can help it," Betty muttered so softly she was overheard only by me.

"Welcome back, Trevor. How about introducing us to your friends." Tom's face wore a look of helplessness even as he attempted a welcoming smile. Tousled hair and dark brows framed cobalt eyes. They were the eyes of a dreamer torn between following his muse and the urgency to reclaim his arm from an aggressive teenager.

Trevor tossed me a wink, amused by Dawn's possessive hold on his partner. He then proceeded with a second round of introductions, saving a polite inquiry about the health of Tom's wife and young son for last.

"Wife? You're married?" With that, Dawn dropped Tom's arm and edged away, transferring her interests to some sketches on the nearest easel.

Annie chimed in. "Three years now. And lucky they are that I'm around to stay with the baby when they want to step out for the evening."

I suspected that the trace of disappointment on Dawn's face would vanish, the moment another nice looking young man crossed her path. Betty read my mind and pulled me aside.

Giving an apologetic laugh, she said, "One reason I brought her on this trip was to get her mind off the boys. It's done that, all right. Unfortunately, she's raised her sights from boys her age to married men. What's a mother to do?"

"You're doing exactly what every desperate parent of a teenager would like to do," I said. "Continue exposing her to new experiences and sooner or later she might find a topic other than men that interests her. Maybe she'll even start thinking about a career."

Betty sighed. "I try to be optimistic. You're an example of the kind of successful woman she should emulate. I hope that she's impressed enough to strive for higher goals. After all, she'll be close your age in another ten years. If she doesn't get her head on straight pretty soon, I'll feel that I haven't been a good mother."

"No danger of that. She's going through a stage that we've all gone through. It's part of growing up."

Trevor had been standing apart, but his grin signaled that he overheard every word we were saying. "If nothing else, Betty, bear in mind that 'Torquaytoons' is always looking for a plot that is both serious and humorous, the kind that everyone can relate to in some way."

Betty laughed. "You're saying that Dawn and I may become cartoon characters?"

"You're in good company, Betty. Sarah's alter ego is our next star. That's what you both get for striking up friendships with strange men. But now that you've entered this land of make-believe, how about a tour of the studio?"

"I'd love that, and so would Dawn."

"Me, too," I added.

Trevor squeezed my elbow, confirmation that I was an honored guest. "Then right this way, ladies. You're about to embark on a journey through the process that Tom and I follow from brainstorm to television screen."

CHAPTER THIRTEEN

Mystical Welsh Traditions

Just as Trevor promised, he and Tom gave us a grand tour of all the technical aspects involved in reproducing their characters on film. After taking us step by step through the animation process, they demonstrated how they developed and incorporated the vocal sound track and musical score into the finished product. By the time we had absorbed most of the basics, Annie had tidied her desk and was donning her coat. Once she and Tom left for home, Trevor had little choice but to invite the three of us remaining to dinner.

Betty tossed me a worried look. "Are you sure you want Dawn and me to come along? You two probably have other plans. We don't want to be a bother."

Trevor dispelled her worry, insisting that we all head for a small, pleasant restaurant around the corner. The food was delicious and the conversation animated, sparked by Trevor's witty stories. I remember that he and I sat very close and that he occasionally reached over to pat my hand. Afterward, I could not recall a single comment that Betty made, only the overt boredom Dawn displayed when interacting with her mother. In contrast, she reacted to everything Trevor or I said with respect, even reverence, the kind observed in a student smitten with her teacher.

As we left the restaurant, Trevor hailed a taxi and instructed the cabbie to deliver the Amblers to their hotel and me to my flat. Although there was nothing in Trevor's parting words to hint that he would call me later in the evening, the look deep in his eyes spoke volumes.

I had slipped into bed and was checking over my schedule for the following day when the phone rang. In the split second it took to lift the receiver, I knew that his voice would be the next sound I heard. "Sarah, I'm sorry things didn't go exactly as planned, but I'll make up for it this weekend."

"I had a lovely time, Trevor, and I know that Betty and Dawn were as impressed with your studio as I am. It's fabulous. And Tom and his mother are ever so nice. No wonder you work well together."

"You're right, Sarah. I couldn't ask for a better partner at work. My career is going at high speed. It's given me just about everything I ever dreamed of having, including television awards. Now all I need is a partner at home to complement my success in the business world."

My heart leaped, but my voice held steady. "A gardener, perhaps?"

His low chuckle sent tingles up my spine. "That's not quite the partner I had in mind. We'll talk about it when you're not obsessed with publicity obligations. Where are they sending you tomorrow?"

With my eyes closed, I imagined him by my side.

"York," I said, wishing I were staying in London. "It's rather a distance, but Elspeth says that the express train will get me there in two hours. Since I'm staying overnight for signings at four different shops, I'll have time to see York Minster. She says it's the most impressive cathedral in England and shouldn't be missed."

"And so it is. You'll have lots to tell me when I pick you up Friday at King's Cross Station. What time does your train get in?"

"You'll pick me up?" That prospect brought a smile to my lips. "That's very kind of you, Trevor. I'd really appreciate that. Getting from Kings Cross to Paddington is a bit confusing."

He was waiting at the end of the platform when my train from York pulled in. True to his word, he eliminated all the confusion in my mind that Elspeth's schedule had churned up. With all the expertise city dwelling had instilled in him, he commandeered my bag and whisked me through the crowded concourse to the taxi stand at the curb. Twenty minutes later, we were at Paddington with only moments to spare before the express to Swansea was scheduled to depart.

We clambered aboard and had scarcely settled ourselves before the railway chef, striking in his official tall hat and harlequin print trousers, presented us with the evening menu. This, Trevor explained, was the dinner run, salvation for residents of mid-Wales whose late office hours in London prevented them from sharing the evening meal with their families and tucking the youngsters into bed.

    After mulling over the entrée options, we both chose fish and chips, my first opportunity to sample the traditional British favorite. While it was being prepared in the adjacent car, the waiter whetted our appetites with a hearty beef vegetable soup and a tomato, cucumber and watercress salad accompanied by a miniature loaf of wheat bread. Unlike the greasy fare plunked into newspaper cones by street vendors, the main dish that followed was crisp and airy, the mark of culinary genius. The meal was topped off by a raspberry tart that was neither too sweet nor too filling. In short, it was simply perfect. As was my company.

    Long after he cleared our dishes, the waiter continued to refill our pot of Earl Grey tea. Lulled by the warm brew and the tranquil scenes hurtling past our window, we exchanged impressions of the two days spent apart from one another. After I described my visits to York Minster and the Viking Museum, Trevor talked about the casting session to choose voice doubles for characters he and Tom were developing and their discussions with the music director about background themes for each. Our conversation was so animated and we were so focused on one another that the train sat in the Swansea station for several minutes before we realized that the passengers and crew had gone and the cleaning crew, armed with waste bins, had boarded, impatient for us to leave. We gathered our belongings and switched to a local platform, barely catching the next train for Carmarthen. Meredith was waiting there to chauffeur us to the cottages.

    "I hope you're in good voice, Sarah," he said.

"Tomorrow is your debut rehearsal."

Trevor gave him a reassuring nod. "Everything is 'Go' from our end. I hope it's the same from yours."

Meredith nodded. "The local constabulary has been notified. They passed along a piece of surveillance equipment, a bracelet for Sarah to wear so she can be traced, if necessary." He sought my eye through the rear view mirror. "I left it on the night stand in the guest cottage. You'll want to wear it to rehearsal tomorrow, just in case."

Trevor frowned. "Just in case? Do the authorities think he'll take the bait right away?"

"They don't know any more than we do. He could be perfectly harmless. On the other hand, there have been eleven victims so far. If one per month is the goal, it's about time for the next."

Trevor sucked in his breath. "That doesn't give us much leeway, does it?"

"Look at it this way," Meredith said. "If the operation works out as planned and Phil is the perpetrator, we'll have him in custody. Then perhaps he'll be persuaded to explain what happened to the victims."

As we drove through the Pembrokeshire villages and countryside less than four hours from the busy transportation hubs of London, I was overcome by an inexplicable serenity, no matter the unknown I faced. Just as the tranquil seacoast invited a peaceful existence, the proximity of the two dependable Evans brothers was quiet confirmation that my safety was their foremost concern.

Trevor and I spent the early part of the evening with his family guffawing over our appearance on the Sophia Rydal Show that his mother taped earlier, but once bedtime arrived for the rambunctious twins, we began a leisurely drive to St. Davids. Despite the late hour, the sun lolled in the western sky, resisting the inevitable drift below the horizon. Our route along the coastal road occasionally drew within view of the Pembrokeshire Path where scattered hikers and bikers were taking advantage of the long daylight hours. By the time we reached the car park serving the cathedral, the sky was fringed by a palette of deep reds and oranges. Even after the sun dropped behind the horizon, an eerie white swatch of twilight lingered over the sea. Momentarily, a curtain of indigo crept westward. As we watched, it enveloped the hills before giving way to the stars poised to prick out one by one across the heavens.

Trevor marked my gasp. "I agree, Sarah. It's a beautiful sight. That streak of white in the sky is typical this time of year. Some believe that it's the spirit of St. Non watching over the holy well."

"Who is St. Non? And where is the holy well?"

"You'll see shortly. That's where I'm taking you."

I looked up into his face and returned his smile. "There seems to be a purpose behind your every move."

He laughed and reached for my hand. "You should know by now, Luv, that we have a magical meeting of the minds. Come along, then. The well is some distance, but we should reach it in time for you to have a glimpse before the light fades completely."

The worn path was crafted of pebbles smoothed

by time. It skirted the deep depression that for centuries secreted the largest cathedral in Wales from sea borne plunderers. Within minutes, we had passed beyond the lights and sounds of the tiny city and were breasting a wind-swept plain of tall grasses and occasional clumps of foxglove. Despite the chilly air, I was warmed by our rapid pace and Trevor's nearness. His hand clasped mine in a firm grip.

By the time we reached a stile barring the pathway from the plain, he had told me the story of St. David, the patron saint of Wales, and the sacred well that erupted nearby at the moment of his birth to the maiden Non and a Welsh chieftain. The sanctity of the well had been proven many times over the centuries, he explained, by the miracles that occurred to those who dipped their hands into its waters.

After helping me across the stile, Trevor pointed to a small excavation. "Just ahead you see what remains of the chapel built in St. Non's honor fourteen centuries ago. Folks believe that it was built on or near the house where St. David was born. For that reason, this is regarded as holy ground. Pilgrims are welcome, but the stile is a barrier to ordinary tourists."

I shivered, not so much from the oppressive wind and the darkening sky but from the feeling that I was in the grip of an arcane spirit. My teeth chattered as I managed, "What an eerie site. No wonder it's held in awe."

He squeezed my hand. "Now that you've seen the chapel and understand its power, I'll take you to the well. It's just a few yards away."

Clinging to his hand, I followed him over the rough ground to a low and unexpected outcropping. As we drew closer, I could hear the faint ripple of water over the rocks.

"Watch your step," Trevor cautioned, as he guided me across slippery boulders to the source. Dropping my hand, he stooped down and let the stream pour freely over his outstretched palms. When he finally stood, he reached for my hands, capturing them both in a firm, icy grip. "Relax, Sarah. Cold water represents truth. I've made my wish. Now it's your turn."

"Is this a wishing well?"

He smiled. "So they say. The only restriction is that your wish must come from the heart."

"That's easy. Mine is definitely from the heart." So saying, I knelt down, closed my eyes, and allowed the water to pour through my fingers. I had expected to be startled by its coldness; instead, a tremendous warmth gushed upward from my feet to the crown of my head. The unexpected sensation so unnerved me that I nearly lost my balance.

Trevor caught me, and drew me to my feet. During the moment we stared deep into the other's eyes, time stood still. I grappled with a lightheaded feeling, an inexplicable flash of giddiness. In the next instant, his arms enfolded me. Our lips met in a kiss that told me nothing else in the world mattered.

At length, he drew back and took a deep breath. "That's what I've wished for since the moment we met, Sarah, my darling."

"Well for goodness sake, Trevor, what took you so long?"

His voice sounded apologetic. "I wanted to be sure that you wanted it too."

"Couldn't you tell?"

"After blurting out that remark about celebrating our fiftieth wedding anniversary, I needed to guard my mouth and my feelings until I was sure we're both on the same wave length."

"We've been on it since that very moment."

"For me the truth came even earlier. I was studying you on the train long before you attacked me. There was something in your face that was endearing, even familiar. I didn't know anything about you, but I felt as if I were being pulled toward you and everything I've dreamed was coming true. I only chased you through Bath, but I would have chased you to the end of the earth if need be. By the time I walked into the green room at the television station, my subconscious was out of control. Even as the words were coming out of my mouth, I was terrified that I'd scared you off."

"Those words made my heart stand still, but not from fright. You intrigued me. The more I learned about you, the more certain I was that I really did want to celebrate my fiftieth wedding anniversary with you."

"And so you shall, my dearest Sarah." He nuzzled my hair, then kissed me again. It was even better the second time.

Later, after we had hugged and kissed again and again and shared the deeply private thoughts that lovers confess at that precious moment of wonderment, we strolled toward the edge of the cliff. By then, the full moon had risen from behind mainland hills and was reflected in the bay. Its brilliance delineated the icy waves crashing far below us against the rocks, a warning in their roar that this wild, primitive land was still gripped in mystery. Buffeted by the wind, Trevor and I held each other close.

Against my ear, he said, "This is where you and I first met."

My head jerked around. "What do you mean? I've never been here in my life."

He gestured broadly, encompassing the western horizon. "You were here in spirit, darling. Don't ask me how or why, but I knew it was merely a matter of time until we met. Do you know the old song that begins, 'My Bonnie Lies over the Ocean?'"

"That takes me back to my childhood. But what does it have to do with…?"

It might have been the middle of the day, so clearly did the moon illuminate the smile on his face. "When I was a tiny lad, I was an inveterate dreamer. Whenever I heard that song I'd tell my parents or teacher that 'My Bonnie' lived on the other side of the ocean and was coming to me one day. As soon as I became old enough to drive, I would come here by myself, dip my hands in the holy well, and wish for her to materialize. I believed she would appear at the right time. And she did."

I shivered in his arms, as if hearing the pronouncement of a great truth. "What if I weren't your 'Bonnie.' What if the real 'Bonnie' has yet to arrive?"

Softly, he said, "You're the only reality I need."

The kiss proved his point.

Early the next morning, I launched a series of interviews with more families of the missing girls. Enid had scheduled them in advance, leaving me nothing to do except dig into the back stories and make note of individual reactions. Between breakfast and lunch, Trevor ferried me to three homes; Enid had scheduled three more for Sunday. The responses from the first three families duplicated those of my two interviews the previous week. The parents welcomed my willingness to delve into the disappearances, but all were uncommonly adamant about Phil. To them, he was a cherished link to their daughters. They recited the sympathetic remarks he made during his visits and the many kindnesses he showed during their time of trial. Not one would accept the suggestion that he — or their daughters' devotion to music — contributed to the tragedy.

Following tea and a few moments to relax and contemplate the day's findings, Trevor delivered me to St. Brynach's Church in Nevern. We arrived a few minutes before Phil's choir rehearsal was scheduled to begin. I wore the electronic bracelet Meredith obtained. Having run through several preliminary tests earlier in the afternoon, I felt fairly secure about its use. To make certain that the system was operating precisely, Trevor and Meredith drove me to a number of places up and down the coast. At times, they secreted me out of doors; other times they planted me inside a building, some occupied, others deserted. No matter how clever or obscure a place they chose, the police radioed them each time within minutes to report my exact location. I was thankful that the police and the bracelet were in sync and completely trustworthy.

Trevor gave me a reassuring hug. "You'll be fine, Sarah. I'll park nearby and pick you up when he dismisses the choir."

I hoped my smile would not divulge my rising apprehension. "Knowing you're outside, I'll focus on the music and think nothing but happy thoughts."

"That's my sweetheart."

His peck on the cheek sent me scurrying down the path where young women, some mere teenagers, others closer my age, were drifting into the chapel, music folders under their arms. Once inside, I hesitated while the others mounted the stairs to join their respective sections in the choir stall. As they viewed me with the universal curiosity a closed society might direct toward an outsider, I returned their guarded smiles and felt the awkward alienation a student feels the first day in a new school.

Presently, Phillip entered from a door behind the choir loft, a stack of music in his arms. Catching sight of me, he immediately placed the pile on the piano bench and came forward to introduce me to the others as "a friend of the Evans family."

With that, the sea of faces regarding me relaxed. My surname gave them further proof that I was not an intruder, but a fellow singer with a Welsh connection. Phil asked me to run through a few scales and I obliged. Visibly pleased by my performance, he smiled and decided aloud that I was perfectly suited for the second soprano section. The entire section moved closer together to provide enough space for me, and several offered to share their music folders.

Phillip shook his finger at them as he handed me a folder stuffed with sheet music. "Sarah has a very strong voice. It's important that she have her own music to study during the week, so I've prepared this for her."

I thanked him for the folder, all the while wanting to melt into the crowd from this point on. That proved to be an easy matter. He quickly shifted the topic to one of the anthems with a difficult alto passage that needed work, and before additional worries overcame me, we were deep into the rehearsal.

For nearly two hours, we took the music apart one measure at a time until each section had mastered its lines. During a brief break, I chatted with those seated nearby, hoping to jog their impressions of Phil. They, however, were more interested in learning about my relationship to the Evans family, Trevor in particular. Sensing that a few of them rather fancied him themselves, I divulged very little, turning the conversation back as best I could to the choir itself to learn more about the members who had disappeared. If they knew more than I had already uncovered, they gave away nothing. Jane, seated to my left, remarked about the selfless comfort Phil gave to the families. That praise drew vigorous nods of approval from Catherine on my right. Clearly, the question of his virtue had no audience among these choir members.

The rehearsal was so rigorous that I welcomed the end. I gathered up my folder and was about to follow those leaving the chapel when I felt someone tap my shoulder. Even before turning around, I knew it was Phil.

"I'm very impressed by your contributions this

evening," he said. "It occurs to me that your voice is solo quality. At the very least, it would blend beautifully and you would hold your own in a small, select group."

"That's very kind." By now he was tugging on my sleeve, leaving me no way to exit gracefully.

"If I may take a moment of your time, I'd like to show you several compositions in my files that would be perfect for your voice range. Come with me back to the storage room. I can put my finger on them in no time."

My heart began to beat faster. I tried to extricate my sleeve from his grip. "Maybe some other time. My friends are waiting and we have plans for the evening."

He released my sleeve, but remained so close I felt his warm breath on my face. "Surely you're not afraid, are you?"

Startled, I managed, "Of course not. Why should I be afraid?"

"Some singers do beautifully performing in a large group, but stage fright overcomes them when they stand before an audience as a soloist."

My rapid heartbeat down shifted. "Oh, I see what you mean. The only solo experience I've had is in school choruses. I don't know how I'd react at this point in my life."

His manufactured smile verged on a leer. "I'm sure that you can carry it off perfectly. Just a moment, then. Please come this way."

By now, the chapel was empty except for the two of us. I glanced toward the entryway, expecting Trevor to be hovering there.

"Come, come," Phil called. He waited, his hand on the knob of the door behind the choir stall. There was nothing for it but to follow.

We entered a small, windowless room remarkable for its orderly disarray. Against two walls were open file drawers of music, their overflow piled in stacks on the floor. The remaining wall space accommodated several racks of choir robes that may have been responsible for the musty smell permeating the air.

I waited alongside the exit door while Phil shuffled through several piles of music until he located three sheets that pleased him. "Here. Take these with you and practice the solo lines until you feel comfortable. If you come early next Saturday, we can go over them together so you get the feel of how they fit with the other voices and the accompaniment."

"I'll do my best, although I can't guarantee that I'll learn them to your satisfaction."

His brittle expression belied the encouragement intended in his response. "You'll be perfect for them. This means that everything is coming together beautifully for our very special performance at the Eisteddfod."

"The Eisteddfod?" I frowned. Could there be a connection between the annual celebration and the missing girls?

He moved toward me slowly, deliberately, waving the music. "We've been working toward it all year. In little more than a month we'll prove ourselves in Aberystwyth before all of Wales. Your voice is the ingredient we've been missing."

What was it that someone – was it Meredith? – had said about Aberystwyth? I reached for the music, but he retained his grip. It occurred to me that he had no intention of allowing me to snatch the music and run. Just as I believed he was considering grabbing me and perhaps suffocating me with a choir robe, a door creaked. At the first footfall, my heart leaped, believing it to be Trevor, but the burly man entering the exit hidden by the rack of robes was a stranger.

CHAPTER FOURTEEN

Holy Grail Connection

Phil gave a start. "Why, Sergeant Floyd. What brings you here?"

The newcomer's gruff voice complemented his thickset body. "Just checking the premises. The antiquity hunters we picked up here last weekend wanted to break into the cave. It's a pity we had to let them go for lack of evidence. If they come back soon – and we believe they will – the chapel would be a good hiding place until the coast is clear. They'd draw attention entering by the main door, but they could sneak in easily through this unlocked rear door." So saying, he fastened it securely with a decisive twist of the latchkey. "We'll leave through the chapel."

"Yes, well, that does seem like a good idea." I tried to ascertain if the tone of Phil's voice registered concern that his own secret access was now blocked temporarily.

The Sergeant turned to me. "You must be Miss Morgan." Without waiting for my response, he opened the door into the chapel and nudged me forward. Halfway down the main aisle, he said, "Trevor Evans is looking for you. He's waiting outside."

A rush of relief crossed Trevor's face when he saw us. With a bound, he was by my side. "I expected you to leave with the others, but you never came. When I went into the chapel looking for you, nobody was there. By the time I came back outside, thinking I'd missed you, Sergeant Floyd had arrived. He told me he was trailing your signal and knew exactly where to find you."

"I've known about the rear entry for years," the sergeant explained. "One stone slab on the outer wall is a hidden door. It can be shoved open easily, unless it's latched from within."

"Then whoever built it must have been deceptive intentionally," I said.

"Absolutely. It was constructed to give pilgrims a secret entryway into the sanctuary and the holy men a means of escaping with the church relics if plunderers arrived."

Trevor's hand was firm on my arm. "Do you think that Phil intended to hold you there?"

Over his shoulder, I saw Phil leave the building. It would not do for him to overhear our conversation. I cleared my throat.

Trevor understood. Aloud he said, "It sounds as if you enjoyed yourself, Sarah. If you're ready to leave, we'll be on our way. Sergeant, I believe you're parked right behind me."

Once we reached our cars, Sergeant Floyd glanced back to confirm that Phil was out of range, then folded his arms across his chest. "Now you can tell us what really happened."

"Truthfully, nothing seemed out of ordinary

during the rehearsal. Phil directed in a very professional manner and avoided showing favoritism toward any of the choir members. Aside from having me audition briefly in front of the others and assigning me to a section, he hardly paid attention to me at all until he dismissed the choir. That's when I became worried. As I was about to leave, he asked me to follow him to the storage room for some solo parts he wants me to practice."

Trevor scratched his head. "Solos? For a newcomer? That puts you in an awkward position."

"Does it ever. It makes me a target, but it also gives me an opportunity to find out what he's up to."

Sergeant Floyd's eyes narrowed. "Did you learn anything that you didn't know before?"

"He said we're rehearsing for the Eisteddfod."

"The entire choir?"

"That was my impression. But what stuck in my mind is that it will be held in Aberystwyth." I turned to Trevor. "Didn't Meredith say the cup is there?"

"Or its facsimile. I can tell you think there's a connection."

"I wouldn't be surprised. Phil showed up right after the police arrested the men looking for the Cross. When the conversation somehow got around to the Holy Grail, he seemed to be upset that Meredith explained the history to Dr. Wilson."

Trevor nodded slowly. "You may be on to something."

At that moment, Sergeant Floyd's mobile rang. The conversation was brief. He checked his watch. "I'm wanted back at headquarters on another matter, but if anything else occurs to you, any connection at all, let me know."

"You can count on it," Trevor said. "And thanks for rescuing Sarah. She might have been perfectly safe alone with Phil, but without the bracelet your department provided, the outcome could have been entirely different."

"Right you are, Mr. Evans. Perhaps she was about to become the next to vanish without a trace."

Before he could walk away, I grabbed his sleeve. "If you're so convinced that Phil had something to do with the missing girls, what has prevented you from taking him in for questioning?"

"Oh we did, Miss Morgan, a number of times, but there wasn't a shred of evidence to prove that they didn't all run away from home. Another brick wall was the faith and trust that their parents have in him. The entire community respects Phil. They admire his musical ability and especially how he goes out of his way to help others. His wife is the same way. Must be a year now that she's been up north tending to a sick relative."

Trevor's head snapped around. "Mrs. Griffith has been gone for a year? How do you know he didn't murder her?"

Sergeant Floyd smiled. "Good question. That's the first thing we wanted to know, but he's in the clear. After all, Mrs. Griffith is a practical nurse. It's only natural that she would be called for a family illness. Phil goes up to visit her during the week, and she telephones her friends here every so often. One of our neighbors heard from her only last week. Said she has to stay on because it looks like the end is coming. She'll be back when it's all over."

"The relative is dying, you mean?"

"Seems so."

Trevor shook his head. "Curious. There's a lot that doesn't add up."

"That's exactly why we're here," Sergeant Floyd said.

The first thing Trevor did when we got back was to question Meredith about the elderly Aberystwyth vicar. Theories aside, there was no clear common bond between him, the Nanteos Cup, and Phil. Both agreed, however, that my newly-christened solo quality voice could be a critical addition to the puzzle.

Although concerns for my safety diminished during the family gathering that evening, a romp with the twins and a carload of laughs provoked by several more episodes of "Torquaytoons," I could not dismiss the persistent aura of foreboding.

The first thing Sunday morning, Trevor and I drove north to Aberystwyth. Our mission was to find clues, but the pleasant seaside town, dominated by its Royal Pier, was not primed to divulge much beyond its white beach dotted with sea birds, several folks on holiday wading tentatively into the cold surf, and the fresh, salty air that accompanied us up the steep streets to the university perched on the crest of a hill.

Ignoring the peal of church bells from all sides beckoning worshipers to spend Sunday morning in prayer, students newly arrived for the summer session were more focused on pursuing their studies on the lawn or in the library where Trevor sought out the reference librarian. His query sent her searching through old documents for mention of the Nanteos Cup. Some time later, she returned from the stacks, apologizing that her efforts were fruitless, but as we turned to leave, she caught Trevor's arm.

"Just a thought," she said. "When I was a wee one, the cup was occasionally a topic around our family table. I didn't pay much attention at the time, but maybe something helpful will come back to me. If you'll leave a number where I can reach you…"

Trevor obliged. After thanking her, we retraced our steps to the town's main thoroughfare where colorful flyers posted at every street corner caught our attention. We stopped beside one to peruse it further.

"I recognize the word 'Eisteddfod,' but the rest is incomprehensible," I said.

Trevor laughed. "It's the Welsh secret code. Broadly translated, the notice says that Aberystwyth residents are reminded to reserve their seats for the most magnificent Eisteddfod ever." He raised his eyebrows. "Time will tell what that implies."

The comments by the families I interviewed in early afternoon varied little from those recorded during my previous five contacts. I thanked each profusely for their willingness to share with a stranger, although none provided clues beyond what I found in the newspaper accounts. I doubted that the two families Enid had scheduled me to meet the next weekend would be any more helpful. Counting my discussion with Enid about her sister, Gwen, those interviews would conclude my meetings with the loved ones of the missing eleven girls.

By mid-afternoon, we congregated around the Evans dinner table, partaking of the Sunday feast Trevor's mother and Enid had prepared. Amid carefree chatter, amply punctuated by Trevor's wit and the twins' cunning antics, we polished off the roast leg of lamb, oven-browned potatoes, minted carrots and peas, garden salad, and yeasty rolls. The final exhibit, a caramel pie with mile-high meringue, shattered my vow to count calories. Once the china, pots and pans were relegated to the dishwasher, we all embarked on a leisurely stroll along the Pembrokeshire Path.

The scent of honeysuckle wafting in from the meadows blended with the sea air, bringing James Russell Lowell's poetic question to mind immediately. Without a doubt, this rare day in June was one of the most perfect I had ever known. The sun beamed down upon the unspoiled seacoast below where children searched for treasures in the sand and fishermen angled from the water's edge for a prize catch. The panorama of sailboats and coracles bobbing on calm waters extended to the farthest horizon. Closer in, the leaping porpoises and bottlenose dolphins drew attentive viewers to the shoreline. The sedentary gray seals lazed across rocky ledges jutting from the rugged cliffs, their jocular barks audible above the roaring surf.

Chattering magpies, tamed over the years by hikers willing to share their lunch scraps, hindered our progress as they tottered across grassy verges and onto the footpath begging for spoils. Rebuffed, they swooped in and out of the high hedges separating the path from adjoining pastures. Infrequent breaks in the foliage revealed flocks of sheep grazing among buttercups. On distant hillocks, sturdy stone farmhouses and barns bespoke antiquity and echoed the gentle beauty of the natural surroundings. The scene filled my heart with unspeakable joy, and when the others rushed out of sight around a bend in the path to keep pace with the romping twins and Trevor drew me into his arms, I closed my eyes to welcome his eager kiss. The day was beyond perfect.

Before leaving the cottage that evening, I laid my electronic bracelet on the dressing table. With the weekend winding down and no more need to look over my shoulder, it was time to get back to the real world, the whirlwind schedule of book signings and a radio appearance during the coming week. This time, Trevor drove me to the Swansea station. We had agreed that I would return to London by myself while he remained in Pembrokeshire overnight, using that opportunity to tell his family about us. Despite our brief acquaintance, their eagerness to include me in family gatherings seemed to signal their approval and acceptance of me as a potential in-law. Still, I knew that Trevor felt obligated to follow the prescribed pattern of his heritage and request their blessing. He would take the express back to London early Monday morning.

Upon reaching my flat, I rang up Elspeth to firm my schedule. I hoped that would be the extent of the conversation, but she persisted.

"How was your weekend, Sarah?"

"Just lovely. I joined a woman's choir and rehearsed with the director some people believe is responsible for the missing girls. This gives me the opportunity to observe his behavior closely and look for clues."

"I smell another best-seller coming up. The business end of your weekend isn't exactly what I meant, though. Don't I detect a romantic lilt in your voice?"

I laughed. "Only if you're determined to find one, Elspeth. Blame that lilt on the Welsh love of singing. There's music wherever you go there, from the rhythm of the waves beating against the beach to the twitter of birds in the trees."

"Twittering birds, indeed. I'm talking about your host, who happens to be the romantic idol of every single woman on this fair island."

"Now, Elspeth. As I told you before, Trevor Evans is a gentleman, an incredible wit, and one of the nicest men I've ever met. Let's leave it at that."

I was thankful that she was not present to see the deep blush rise on my face at the mention of Trevor's name and to hear my pounding heart. The time would come when I would have to admit our secret, but there was no hurry. That very quality of friendly openness that I had liked from the moment I met Elspeth also gave me pause. Savvy businesswoman that she was, I feared she could not resist sharing a client's romantic secrets with friends in the press. At best, the pairing of her client with Evans of 'Torquaytoons' fame would enhance my allure and her stature; at worst, the unwanted publicity could sweep away Trevor's privacy.

I spent the better part of the next few days on trains, scurrying to fulfill Elspeth's schedule of book signings in the cities of Leicester, Nottingham, Leeds, and in the London suburb of Reigate. The latter, she prepped me, was utterly upscale and populated by some of the country's most avid readers. At another time, the tight routine might have been oppressive, but I breezed through as if walking on air, all because of Trevor's phone call Monday evening.

"Am I speaking to the future Mrs. Trevor Evans?" he began.

"Oh, Trevor, I hope so. How did they take it?"

"Take it? With open arms. They love you almost as much as I do. Mum's so happy that she's taking the guest cottage off the market and wants to re-decorate it to suit us. Meredith and Enid can't wait for us to marry. Do you suppose they're plotting to add us to their pool of baby sitters?"

I giggled. "That would be fun. The twins are adorable."

"And frisky. Let's hope they calm down before ours arrive."

"You're rushing ahead of me, Trevor."

His voice reflected the cheery smile I loved so dearly. "We'll suit your pace, if that's your desire."

My desire at the moment was to hug him to bits. "I have no problem with an accelerated schedule. It's just that you took me by surprise for a moment. Like you did in the TV studio."

He laughed. "The devil that took control of my tongue that day laid out my entire agenda, Sarah. The sooner we marry, the sooner we can start enjoying a long, leisurely life together."

"That sounds heavenly."

Before blowing kisses to one another over the phone, we arranged to meet at the BBC studio where I would have a radio interview later in the week.

To my dismay, Elspeth was the only familiar face waiting when I arrived. "Tara, bless you, you're right on time." She leaped from the leather chair in the waiting room, instantly towering above the dapper, bespectacled gentleman standing at her side. "You must meet Avery Brown, the host of 'Between the Covers.' You two are bound to have a marvelous chat."

"Delighted to have you on the show, Miss Tyler. I've read your book and I dare say that our listeners will find it every bit as compelling as I did. You've made an excellent case for digging into the records and righting some of the wrongs doled out by courts and jurists who didn't do their homework." He glanced at his watch. "If Miss Wentworth will excuse us, we'll step into the studio and take a few minutes to jot down talking points before going on the air."

Unlike Sophia Rydal, Avery Brown had a solid understanding of my book and the detailed research involved. Although his program was geared toward an educated, literary audience, he never spoke over the head of the average listener. From my vantage point, our conversation had all the elements of a friendly fireside chat and I believed that it would come across in exactly that way to those receiving the broadcast in their homes or on the car radio. Elspeth must have heard it over the waiting room loudspeakers because she was beaming when I emerged from the studio.

"Brilliant, Tara. Your voice and manner came

across like a charm. I can envision hundreds of listeners running out to buy your book."

Avery Brown came up behind me. "And well they should. Miss Tyler took a scholarly approach in her research, but her writing is accessible to everyone. We British like nothing better than a good mystery, especially one that took a century to solve."

Elspeth, her eyes dancing, lowered her voice, as if about to reveal a secret. "You can count on Tara to keep readers happy. She's working on her next mystery even as we speak."

Avery peered at me over the rim of his glasses. "Something to do with BBC?"

I shook my head. "Only indirectly, in that the event may have been covered by your staff. And contrary to what Elspeth would like to believe, I'm not in the process of writing yet, merely sorting out clues."

"If it turns out as well as *The Rittenhouse Murder*, I'll insist on having you back the moment it's published."

"I'll be honored," I told him, as he shook my hand.

Even before Avery excused himself and returned to his office, the knot in my stomach reappeared. Trevor had promised to meet me at the studio. What could have delayed him?

"Here we are." Elspeth dug into her briefcase for copies of my book and a list of a dozen or so unfamiliar names. "Several staff members here begged me to bring along books for you to sign. If this young lady will clear a table for us…"

The receptionist, responding to Elspeth's hint,

leaped to her feet and obliged us by removing some clutter from an adjacent desk and outfitting us with a handful of pens. Just as I placed my signature on the final book in the stack, the door opened and Trevor entered. He was not alone.

CHAPTER FIFTEEN

The Abduction

Trevor's eyes conveyed his apology. "Sorry I'm late, Sarah. Betty rang me up an hour ago. She's in a bit of a bind and needs our help."

Betty Ambler's face was ashen. The crumpled tissue in her fist was no longer useful. Elspeth evaluated the situation at a glance. She snatched an entire box of tissues from atop the receptionist's desk and handed it to Betty.

I hurried to Betty's side. "Where's Dawn?"

My words launched a flood of tears.

"Th…th…that's the problem. I don't know."

Trevor helped her into an easy chair, then took me aside. "Little Miss Mischief has gone in search of Robbie Douglas."

"I haven't the vaguest idea who that is."

"Virgil's drummer."

"Virgil?"

"Sorry. You know him as Clyde Dale."

I stifled a laugh. "How could I forget. But surely you're joking."

"Sad to say, this is not a plot for 'Torquaytoons.' This is a mother's nightmare."

That wiped the smile off my face. "Forgive me, Trevor. What you were saying seemed beyond absurd. I can't believe that Dawn would wander away in a strange city to look for a rock musician. How could she begin to guess where he is? And how can we help Betty find her?"

"We're in luck on that score. After making a couple of calls, I was directed to Virgil's agent. She gave me his phone number and also his schedule. It's fortunate that they're playing in London this week and not out of town. He wasn't home, so I left a message. Since he may not respond until the spirit moves him, our best bet is to go directly to the club. The plans I had for us this evening will have to wait."

Trevor's set jaw confirmed his command of the situation. Few men I knew would undertake such stiff responsibility for mere acquaintances. Without thinking, I put my hand on his arm and murmured something about how proud he made me. Elspeth must have been waiting for me to err in that direction because the next thing I knew she had sidled up to Trevor, her eyes gleaming in anticipation of a scoop.

"Elspeth Wentworth here, Evans. I recognized you right away and can't begin to tell you how much I adore 'Torquaytoons.'"

When Trevor smiled down on her, I was amused to see her eyelids flutter, proof that her professional exterior was cracking. "Delighted to meet the brains behind Sarah's tour," he said, giving her outstretched hand a firm shake.

Elspeth, smitten by his charm, fumbled to make

conversation. "I must thank you for the kindness you've shown Sarah. From what she tells me, her next book will owe a great debt to you."

Trevor's expression was noncommittal, as was his reply. "Her topic is of great interest in my corner of Wales. She's more than welcome to whatever help my family and I can give."

Elspeth, I feared, would have chatted him up at length to coax a confession and meaty details of our relationship, but he was a veteran of media pressure and knew precisely how to handle her inquisitiveness. After a brief exchange, he explained our concern about Betty's daughter. "Since we're the only people she knows here, and I have a lead to Dawn's whereabouts, we must press on without further delay," he said.

Elspeth's face did not disguise her disappointment, but she stepped aside with typical British grit, saying, "Please don't let me detain you. I understand completely." Turning to me, she added, "We'll be in touch, Sarah. Next week's schedule is very heavy."

Once we saw Elspeth off in a cab, Trevor hailed another for the three of us and directed the driver to the club where Clyde Dale and his band were appearing. During the ride, Betty explained that the trouble erupted during afternoon tea at Brown's.

"Dawn told me that Robbie Douglas gave her his mobile number the day she met him on the television show in Bristol and asked her to get in touch when she got to London. Apparently she called him several times secretly. When she told me he'd invited her to tonight's show, I made it very clear that I brought her on this trip to acquaint her with British culture, not rock musicians."

"I should hope not," I said, ignoring the irony of the situation as my conscience reminded me that I, too, had been swept off my feet soon after arriving in England, although not by a rock musician. "How did she react?"

"She began to argue, and when I tried to quiet her down to avoid making a scene in the restaurant, she said she would go by herself. Just as the server brought our bill, Dawn jumped up from her chair. I thought she was going to the ladies' room. It was quite a bit later that someone remembered seeing her leave the restaurant. She must have known where he's playing, but I didn't, and I had no idea how to get in touch with anyone except you two. If it weren't for Trevor I'd be at a complete loss about where to begin."

"Trevor will find her. He's a font of information, and he has the most amazing power of persuasion of anyone I've ever known," I said.

Trevor's hand sought mine and squeezed it warmly, reassurance that there would be a happy ending to Dawn's disappearance.

The cabbie pulled up before a trendy club. Even though it was late afternoon, avid Clyde Dale fans already were queued behind a brass rail to await the evening performance. Betty and I followed tentatively as Trevor, not intimidated by the enormous 'SOLD OUT' banner, walked briskly to box office and pounded on the window. Moments later, a beaming manager appeared from a side door, shook Trevor's hand, and motioned us inside.

As he led us into the main performance area, a condensed theater-in-the-round, my hands flew to my ears. The manager shouted to us something about a sound check, scarcely making himself heard above the din.

Clyde at the piano dominated center stage. The other members of his band gyrated back and forth, each improvising on his own instrument, none more aggressively than Robbie Douglas on drums.

It was impossible to hear the manager's next remark, but when he pointed to a small figure sitting in a far corner, Betty's whoop drowned out the band. She would have run to Dawn had not Trevor grabbed her arm and signaled her to be discreet.

At length, the number ended and we caught Clyde's eye. Instead of the bold yellow cape he had worn to the television studio, he, like the other musicians, could have passed for any laboring man attired in well-worn jeans and tee shirt. Still, casual dress could not subdue his overt personality. The moment he recognized Trevor, he leaped from the stage.

"Evans, my man, you've brought that delectable American writer." His face twisted into an elfin grin. "The way you were cozying up to her on the couch, I suspected you had more on your mind than cartoons."

Trevor laughed, neither admitting nor denying our romance. "It's always a pleasure to see you, Virgie. Sarah and I couldn't resist catching your show while she's in town. And you remember her friend, Betty Ambler. She and her daughter were in the Bristol audience."

Virgie, alias Clyde, grabbed Betty's hand and

mine and kissed them both. "You three will be my special guests this evening."

"Actually, there are four of us," Trevor said.

Virgie stopped in the midst of a second round of hand-kissing. "Four? Are you being hounded by a ghost?"

"Nothing like that, even if the Tower of London is just around the corner." Trevor gestured toward Dawn, who by now had seen us and was cowering in her seat, not certain whether to run or submit to the punishment. "The fourth is sitting over there. She's Betty's daughter, Dawn. I believe she was invited here by Robbie Douglas."

Virgie's eyes popped open even wider. He lowered his voice. "She's under age?"

Trevor nodded. "That's about the sum of things, Virgie. We've come to rescue her from temptation, but we'd like to do it without making a scene or giving her cause to rebel. It'll be a few hours before you go on. That gives us time to get something to eat. We'll come back for the show, but only for the first half."

"Splendiferous," Virgie said. "Whatever works for you. Would it help matters if we all went to dinner together? That way, she can chat with Robbie in a supervised setting." He lowered his voice to a near-whisper. "Actually, he's a very shallow conversationalist. She'll probably pick up on that right away. By the time she sits through dinner with him and half of our show, she'll be ready to forget about him."

Even Betty laughed at that. Linking arms with her, Virgie pranced across the room to Dawn. Trevor winked at me as we followed behind.

"It's a royal occasion when my old buddy Evans brings his glamorous friends to our gig." Virgie gave Betty a bear hug for Dawn's benefit. "We're popping out for a bite before the show. You'll join us, of course, Dawn?"

Dawn regarded the two of them warily, no doubt wondering when the ax would fall. As it slowly became clear to her that Betty was agreeable to the arrangement, she ventured a weak smile and nodded.

Virgie rubbed his hands together and executed the signature playful leap and click of the heels that set his fans screaming for more. "Super! I'll round up some of the boys and we'll dash around the corner to a great little pub that serves the best steak and kidney pie ever, if you like that sort of thing." He rolled his eyes. "Oh ho, Dawn. I see that face you're making. Not to worry, Luv. The cook knows how to broil a decent burger, if that's your cup of tea."

Our mission settled, we trooped over to the pub and slipped into two adjacent booths, Betty, Virgie, Trevor and I in one, Dawn, Robbie, and Hugh the guitarist in the other. By the time we consumed the dishes set before us, the once-animated voices in the next booth had acquired a tinge of boredom. Virgie's assessment of Robbie's conversational appeal had been accurate. Back in the club, once the first set ended and Trevor informed Dawn that we were leaving, she accepted reality.

As we waited outside for the doorman to hail our separate cabs, Dawn looked up at Trevor with an apologetic grin. "It's been a very nice evening, but I didn't know that you and Sarah were coming."

Although he looked at her sternly, I detected kindly humor behind his words. "Neither did we. I hope, young lady, that you understand the seriousness of what you did and that this little caper is the one and only your mother will have to put up with during your trip. You're in a foreign country and you need to behave with caution. Especially where strange men are concerned."

Dawn gulped.

Betty, standing behind her, cast Trevor a grateful glance. "I think we've had our share of London. Perhaps we should spend some time in the countryside."

Not realizing where my enthusiasm would take us, I gushed, "That's a wonderful idea. London is exciting and I hear that English gardens are the finest in the world, but nothing could be lovelier than Wales. The history and beauty are overwhelming."

Betty thought a moment. "A marvelous suggestion, but I don't have any information about hotels in Wales. Where might we stay there?"

Trevor hesitated only seconds before his generous self prevailed. "The cottage where Sarah is staying has three large bedrooms. There's plenty of room for you and Dawn if you'd like to come with us tomorrow."

Betty's face brightened, as if she had just been relieved of a mighty weight. "Oh, could we? Would you mind terribly if we took you up on that? You've been so kind to us, but I hate to be a burden."

"No burden. We'll be glad to have you along and treat you to another aspect of life on this special island."

So it was that Betty and Dawn checked out of their hotel Saturday morning and joined Trevor and me on the express train from Paddington Station to Swansea. This time, Enid met us in the larger family car. Trevor's Mum was watching the twins, so Enid took advantage of her freedom, stopping at every quaint shop we passed to give Betty and Dawn a taste of Welsh culture and herself a rare opportunity to browse without the need to hover over tiny hands capable of mass destruction. It was mid afternoon when we pulled up before the cottages, just as Meredith was parking his car.

He bounded over and gave Enid a peck on the cheek through the open window. "I'll pick up the twins to give Mum a break while she's preparing tea."

"Would you, darling? That will give me time to freshen up."

Trevor caught Meredith on the shoulder, "Before you disappear, how about a hand with the ladies' luggage? We have two more guests this weekend."

Meredith looked a question.

"Friends of Sarah," Trevor said.

Meredith nodded, in receipt of his brother's silent message.

Betty and Dawn, dashing ahead of their hosts, swept through the guest cottage like children in a toy store, admiring the furniture, knick-knacks, and the panoramic view of the countryside. They exclaimed over the farms visible through the kitchen window and the unexpected contrast with the Pembrokeshire Path and the sea beyond. Throughout the cottage, open windows admitted the heady bouquet of herbs and roses and the shrill cries of magpies. Except for the occasional glimpse of hikers on the distant path, we could have been caught in a century-old time warp.

"This is simply enchanting," Betty murmured. "Exactly what we need to calm our nerves."

Just then, Dawn emerged from my bedroom, the electronic bracelet dangling from her fingers. "This is a neat watch. How does it work?"

"It's not a watch. It's a kind of sensor," I said. "I'll explain about it later, but for now we'd better hurry on down to Trevor's Mum's cottage. Her tea is to die for."

Nothing I said could have prepared Betty and Dawn for the veritable feast that the Welsh wave off as a simple prelude to the evening meal. They sampled, raved in superlatives, and sampled some more. Afterwards, sated, we all strolled along the Pembrokeshire Path. Below us, immense waves thundered against the cliffs, the barking seals disciplined their pups, and the coracles of fishermen in quest of sewin for the evening meal bobbed fearlessly on the water. Betty gasped at the beauty stretching before us in all directions and poked Dawn at every turn to make certain her daughter was absorbing the new and exotic sights. I was enjoying the view every bit as much as I had the first time Trevor accompanied me along the path, so it was not until he consulted his watch that I realized it was nearly time for rehearsal.

"You'll have to excuse us," I told Betty. "We'll be back in a few hours. Feel free to drink in some more nature as long as you like. Or maybe you'd rather head back to the cottage to relax."

"Would you mind terribly if Dawn and I tagged along? I'd love to see the village of Nevern. Enid told me it's very historic."

"Why not? While I'm singing, Trevor can explain the stories behind the chapel, and if there's time, you can walk along the stretch of the Pembrokeshire Path that runs behind it." I tried to speak cheerfully and quash my selfish side that had looked forward to the short drive to Nevern with Trevor. Alone.

Trevor's expression confirmed that we were on the same wave length, but his gallantry prevailed. Momentarily, all four of us scrambled into his car, Betty and Dawn into the back seat, I in the passenger seat alongside Trevor. Along the way, Betty chatted non-stop, inquiring about all the places we passed, while Dawn slumped sullenly in the corner, perking up only when we passed a carload of young men.

Singers were already arriving as Trevor parked the car across from the chapel. "Sorry we're a bit tardy, but maybe it's all for the best," he said. I sensed that he had deliberately driven at a slow pace so I would not have to go over my solos with Phil in an empty chapel.

Our eyes met. "There's strength in numbers," I said.

"Exactly. Be careful, Sarah. While you're rehearsing, we'll look around the village. It shouldn't take long, but in case we're not back by the time you're dismissed, wait here in the car."

As Betty and Dawn began walking down the lane toward the village, he put his arms around me and gave me a kiss that reverberated down to my toes. "Mmmm," I sighed. "Is that a prelude to the evening?"

Devils danced in his eyes. "Don't I wish. With the Amblers here, I don't foresee much time alone with you this weekend."

"I'll take whatever is available."

"That's my darling."

Savoring the memory of his kiss, I watched him go before hurrying into the chapel, breathless with apologies for being late. Phil glanced at his watch. "The others are arriving, so there's no time now to hear your solo passages. We'll have a run-through afterwards."

That sent a twinge of fear coursing up my spine.

Once rehearsal began, I felt ill equipped to emulate the other young women seated in my section. Their beautiful voices reflected a lifetime of singing for the sheer love of it. When all parts joined together, soaring above the piano accompaniment, the chapel walls resounded with a fervor to match that of the men's choir. The total effect was spellbinding. Drawn by the glorious sound pouring onto the evening breeze, occasional passersby poked their heads through the open door. Some slipped into rear pews, pausing for a few minutes to drink in the delicious harmonies, tiptoeing away when Phil signaled a break to perfect a line that he felt needed work. He moved through each passage meticulously, perfecting pitch, phrasing, texture, and volume by listening to the members of all sections in groups of two or four. Individual voices stood out, most far superior to mine. All the more reason to be suspicious of his motives.

The dreaded moment arrived as the last few choir members trailed away. We were breaking a good half hour early, Phil explained, because of our excellent progress. As his eyes fell on me, I stiffened and glanced at my watch, hoping that Trevor was receiving my mental plea to return quickly. Only at that moment did I realize my other wrist was bare. The electronic bracelet the police provided must still be lying on the dresser top.

I didn't know whether to blame myself or Dawn. When she asked about it earlier, I remembered being torn between describing its purpose and deliberately withholding something that she and her mother need not know. I chose the latter option, planning to retrieve it when their attention was focused elsewhere; now I would rue my error.

Phil, his arms laden with the collected chorus folders, was summoning me to open the door to the back storage room. I hurried forward at his bidding. Once he passed through, I followed.

He let the folders fall noisily onto a table top and crooked a finger. "Over here, Miss Morgan. Please be so kind as to stack these in four separate piles while I locate some organ music for tomorrow's service. I'll be just a minute. Then we'll work on your solos."

My chore completed, I edged closer to the door that I had left ajar for a fast escape. My concern was unfounded, for he soon finished rummaging in the closet and emerged with several sheets of music and a bulging paper sack. His hands occupied, he swept past me and back into the chapel.

"Close the door and come along," he called over his shoulder. By the time I drew near, he had settled himself on the piano bench, the music and sack at one end. "I've canceled my men's choir this evening. A brief rehearsal before tomorrow's service should be sufficient. They've worked hard this year and it shows. They're more than ready for the Eisteddfod next month. It should be an easy win."

"They're marvelous. I can't imagine improving on the performance I attended. How many other groups are performing at the Eisteddfod?"

"I'll have no idea until I see the complete program. The choruses and soloists come from all over Wales and the continent. There are even entrants from Welsh communities in North and South America. And of course the musicians make up only part of the event. The writers of poetry and prose are also very competitive."

"It sounds like the experience of a lifetime."

His eyes narrowed. "As it will be for you. And for me. What good fortune that I found you in time to include you in the program." By now, he was playing the introduction to the piece. Several measures before my solo passage, he began to sing the harmonizing line. A nod of his head signaled my entrance.

I responded to the best of my ability, plainly aware that my voice was not on a par with those of the other women. Suspicion about Phil's intentions soared. At length, he expressed satisfaction with my performance. Not waiting for him to lower the music rack, cover the piano keys, and gather his materials, I started toward the door in search of Trevor. I had gone only a few steps when I felt Phil's hand clutch my shoulder.

He must have interpreted my gasp as one of fear, for he laughed and clucked his tongue. "Now, now, now.

Why are you jumping?"

"No reason except that old churches sometimes have a spooky aura. For a moment, I mistook you for a spirit from the past."

"Astounding. So you *do* feel a link with antiquity." Before I could answer, he continued. "The moment we met I sensed your connection with the gentle druids, the forest spirits who guide us still. That brings to mind another piece of music that would be perfect for you. I believe it's in my car. Please follow me. I'm parked on the lane."

I quit the chapel gladly, wishing Phil could be dismissed with equal haste. My eyes flew to Trevor's car parked across the road, expecting to see him and the others waiting inside, but it was empty. I concluded that they were drawn to the Pembrokeshire Path after touring the village. After all, they could not have known that the rehearsal ended much earlier than scheduled.

Phil hurried around the side of the church to his car. I stayed several steps behind. From that vantage point, I had a clear view of the Path, no more than fifty yards distant. Several joggers crossed my vision, but there was no sign of Trevor, Betty, and Dawn. I slowed my pace, wishing for a reason to flee in the opposite direction. Phil leaned into the back seat of his car. He appeared to be puttering through a pile of music, but hastily straightened himself as my footsteps on the gravel announced my approach.

"Here's what I wanted," he said. "Come, take a look."

In one unbroken movement, he grabbed my arm, shoved me onto the back seat, and thrust a sheet of music into my hand. "This is a beautiful, ethereal piece, perfect for your voice." He began to hum the melody, all the while maintaining a firm grip that kept me off balance, unable to rise.

Naked fear coursed through my veins like the onrush of an icy liquid. Outwardly, I assumed a mask of serenity. "It's lovely. I'll work on it during the week."

"Splendid, but before you go, you need to know the background of the piece. That will help you get into the spirit of the occasion. It's based on the ancient Welsh legend of the twelve maidens raised in the forest by druids."

"I'm not familiar with that story." I flexed my shoulder to disengage his hand.

His grip tightened. "Then I must explain it. Otherwise, you won't be able to interpret the music properly. Each maiden, one for every month of the year, represents a plant or creature of the forest and embodies its purest qualities. For instance, the violet is beautiful, the fern is shy, the willow is graceful, the dove is gentle, the faun is trusting, and the rabbit is joyful. Their hearts are coveted by humans who fancy themselves in love with the maidens, but the wise druids know that the maidens, if taken from their woodland home, will be corrupted by man. To preserve their purity, they lead the maidens deep into the forest to a secret cave where they feast on ambrosia of the gods and the music of the spheres until they become one with nature."

As he narrated the legend, Phil gradually released the pressure on my arm, but his eyes were riveted on mine in a hypnotic stare. Somewhere beyond his droning voice, unexpected sounds played games with my consciousness: the crackle of paper, a metal container uncapped. The rush of a sweet, strange odor I could not identify overwhelmed me. My eyelids drooped. I fought to rise, but my legs were leaden. The last thing I remember is the pressure of a wet sponge against my nose and mouth and a futile struggle to breathe.

CHAPTER SIXTEEN

The Twelfth Victim

I awoke on a rough pallet. My hands dangled over the edges onto a damp, earthen floor They were numb and unresponsive to signals from my brain urging me to sit up. I squeezed my fingers repeatedly against my palms until the numbness faded and feeling began to return. Using my hands as props, I rose to a sitting position. Now able to stretch forward, I grabbed my feet and kneaded them until circulation was restored. Once my extremities were operating, I became aware of my temples pulsating, as if a tight rubber band encircled my forehead. But when I touched my brow, nothing was there.

I opened my eyes slowly to a black void. Soon I became aware of soft murmurs all about and the sound of someone striking a match. Momentarily, a tiny flame flared in the far corner. As my eyes began to adjust to the gloom, I perceived moving shapes. One inched toward me. When it was no more than an arm's length away, I was able to make out the face of a young woman.

"You're the last one," she said. Her voice held a smidgeon of relief.

"The last one? What do you mean?"

"You're number twelve. The final forest maiden. Now he's happy."

"You mean Phil?"

"Mr. Griffith? Yes. He has all he needs."

"For what?"

"For the Eisteddfod."

I tried to clear my head. "Tell me who you are and exactly what is going on."

She sat down on the floor next to me, tailor fashion. As she did, other figures began to materialize. They had been there all along. "My name is Gwen Edwards."

My heart jumped. "Gwen? Are you Enid's sister? Enid Evans?"

"Yes." Her next words came in a rush. "You know Enid? How is she holding up?"

"She's been worried sick, but the family has never given up hope."

"I can't say the same for those of us here. It's been a long ordeal, especially for the ones taken first."

I glanced up at the others encircling me. "Tell me your names."

Susan Jones. Margaret Davis. One by one they responded right down to the very last name on the list I compiled at the newspaper office.

"Then you're all safe. Have you any idea where we are?"

Gwen shook her head. "None of us saw where he brought us. The only thing we know for certain is that we're underground far enough so that the temperature remains constant throughout the seasons. It could be a cave, or it could be part of another structure, perhaps a dungeon in one of the ancient castles."

"This is the only room?"

"No. This is where we sleep. When it's time to eat, Laura unlocks the door and we follow her through several tunnels to the kitchen. We sit on benches at a long, wooden table."

"Laura?"

"Laura Griffith. Phil's wife."

"The police think that she's taking care of a sick relative up north."

"That's impossible. She watches over us day and night."

"But how does she detain you? She's just one person. Since she's outnumbered, you should be able to overpower her."

"We've thought about that, believe me," Susan said. "To begin with, Laura's built like a pugilist. She's very tall and powerful as a tank, qualities needed by a practical nurse who lifts patients and turns mattresses. I'm sure she'd have no qualms about using them to subdue anyone foolhardy enough to attack her. And then, of course, she has an ample supply of chloroform."

"Chloroform? Why, that must be what knocked me out."

"There's plenty more where that came from," Gwen assured me. "We all ended up here exactly the same way. Phil ran into us on the Pembrokeshire Path, supposedly by accident. He convinced each one to follow him back to the church with the offer of a solo in the Eisteddfod. When we got there, he remembered that the music was in his car and while we were studying it, he knocked us out with the chloroform."

"So that's how he managed," I said. "Everyone wondered why you all were last seen on the Path."

"Now that we're trapped, here, he holds the threat of death over our heads if we don't sing to please him. When Susan started to rebel during rehearsal one day, he told her she was asking to be eliminated once and for all, implying that he would give her enough to kill her."

Without hesitation, I said, "He's a madman."

"We figured that out a long time ago. He has a very small build for a man, so it wouldn't be hard for us to overcome him without the chloroform and his wife in the picture, but they're only part of the problem. Even if we could break away, we might run in the wrong direction and go deeper into the ground. All we know is this room, the kitchen, and the music room…"

"The music room?"

"Yes. We rehearse there."

"Where is it located?"

Gwen made a despairing gesture. "It's hard to say. To get there, Laura leads us through a long, winding tunnel at the other end of the kitchen. We spend most of the day there either singing or listening to tapes that are played from the time we awake until we go to sleep."

"That's done so we don't forget our mission," Margaret chimed in.

"Your mission?"

"As the counterparts of the twelve forest maidens representing purity, Phil is planning for us to suddenly appear from the woods encircling the Eisteddfod stage.

He's convinced that the moment we begin to sing, many in the audience will be so shocked that they'll faint away."

"That's absurd. Why does he believe that will happen?"

"He claims that man is naturally evil, and he says that when the sinners in the audience hear the ethereal sound we produce and pass out because of its beauty, they will be cleansed of evil. He told us that his purpose on earth is to take away the sins of mankind through music"

Gwen gave a sarcastic laugh. "It never crosses his mind that he has done evil."

"Of the worst kind, taking you away from your families without any word, and holding you prisoner here for weeks and months on end," I said. "Surely you've tried to escape?"

"Perhaps escape would be more likely if we weren't strung together every time we leave this room."

"Strung together?"

"Yes, and you'll be added to the chain when she comes to take us to breakfast."

"Like a prison chain gang?"

"Exactly. We wear these gowns all the time. Phil says it's the kind of garment the druids wore. The only difference is that the belt around our waist is a thin chain instead of a willow branch. When we move from one area to another, Laura clips a longer chain onto it so that we're attached one to another."

"What do you do about bathing?"

"We manage, after a fashion." Gwen gestured

toward the far corner. There's a very crude version of a bathroom on the other side of the wall with a steady stream of water flowing through a sluice below the floor level. That's where we bathe. The best we can do is what my grandmother used to call a sponge bath."

I perked up. "That water has to be coming from an underground river. If you could follow it, you might eventually see daylight. But I gather that the opening is too narrow for anyone to slip through."

"Yes, we thought of that. It would be impossible."

"Do you suppose the Griffiths constructed the bathroom?"

"Oh, no. This is part of a very early home. The ancient people often adapted caves into living quarters. For all we know, this place antedates the Romans."

"But men had to eat no matter when they lived. Tell me about the kitchen facilities. What kind of food does Laura prepare?"

"We have mostly soups and stews for lunch and supper, oatmeal and other kinds of grain for breakfast. There's tea every day and occasional fruit. She cooks on a very crude wood stove."

I frowned. "It must have some kind of exhaust system."

"There's a flue going up into the ceiling."

"Well then, you can't be terribly deep in the ground. The exhaust has to open into the outdoors. Otherwise you'd all be asphyxiated."

Everyone nodded. Margaret was about to say something, when a distant thud cut into the silence. It was followed by another. Then another. After a short pause, we heard the crack of wood splintering, as if battered by a heavy object. Those who had been standing quickly dropped onto their haunches, cowering as the thuds came closer. They were accompanied by voices growing louder by the second. Gripped by a healthy mixture of fear and expectation, we watched the heavy oak door shudder from the force outside.

Suddenly it gave way. For several seconds we were blinded by the glare of flashlights probing into all corners of our cell, and then a cheer erupted. A chorus of male voices extending far into the tunnel blended with the relieved cries of twelve young women rushing toward the door.

Someone shouted, "They're here! Give us a hand!"

Cheerfully coaxing us along, the men propelled us through the passageway, their lights flickering against the walls and ceiling in search of the next circuitous turn. Any other time, it might have been difficult keeping up with their bold strides, but now I fairly flew along the earthen surface. My eyes on the moving bodies up ahead, I paid scant attention when we broke into larger areas, recognizing the kitchen by the long wooden table Gwen had mentioned and the music room by the harpsichord to accompany the singers. At the time, I did not pause to wonder why a valuable instrument was in a cave. My only goal was to escape into fresh air.

Once we left the music room, I noticed that those walking ahead of us appeared to be ascending a ramp. Voices echoing back down the corridor mingled with the distant roar of engines, and as we twisted around the final curve and neared the end of the passageway, I was blinded by the whirring dome lights of fire engines, ambulances, and police cars encircling the entry. The camera flash lamp in my face did little to improve my vision, but there was no mistaking Trevor's voice calling my name and, before I could react, the warmth of his arms around me.

Without warning, I began to sob, releasing the fear that had welled inside me. It was impossible to stop crying, no matter the gentle and loving words he whispered in my ear. And so he stroked my hair, covered my face with kisses, and rocked me like a baby until the trembling abated and the last salty tear rolled down my cheek.

"I'm so sorry," I said, between sniffles. "I didn't mean to lose it."

He handed me a tissue. "'Sorry' couldn't begin to explain my feelings if anything had happened to you. You're welcome to cry away to your heart's desire, just so long as you're safe and promise to never again give me such a scare."

Another ripple of fear coursed up my spine. "Phil. What about Phil? He must be a maniac. His wife, too."

"They were being escorted into police cars the last I saw. By now, they're well on their way to jail."

"And the girls. Do their families know they've been found?"

"The police are tending to that as we speak. I understand that they'll be taken to the local hospital and examined for any health problems, but I'm sure they'll be released very quickly. Their families can meet them there."

Even as we watched, an ambulance rolled away with the first group, followed by a truck belonging to a television crew.

"This will be a huge scoop for Meredith. Does he know about it?"

Trevor roared. "Know about it? He's right here in the thick of it. Look over there. He's with Gwen."

Meredith had placed his jacket around Gwen to protect her from the chilly night air and was talking animatedly into his mobile. By the time we reached him, he was beaming. "As soon as I talked with the office and filed my report, I called Enid and told her I'm coming home with the biggest surprise of her life."

"Does she know what it is?"

"She must. The sound of my voice and the background noise surely gave it away, but she didn't press me for details. Whatever she felt in her heart, she was afraid to ask for fear it wasn't true. I can hardly wait to see her reaction when Gwen walks in."

"Then Gwen's not going to the hospital with the others?"

Gwen shook her head vigorously. "Absolutely not. What I need is my family, warm clothes, a soft bed, and a hot meal. But please, no soup or stews."

Meredith laughed. "I'll advise the cook the minute we get back. If it weren't so late, you could call your fiancé."

"Late or not, I intend to call him this very minute, if you'll be so kind as to hand me your mobile."

"I can't think of a better use for it," Meredith

said. He thrust his phone into Gwen's hands and she began dialing immediately. "Still remember his number?"

Gwen looked up, smiling. "I thought about it every hour I was away. It's my lucky number."

Within seconds, the connection went through and with a joyful cry, she began talking with the man whose memory sustained her all those weeks.

Trevor put his arm around my shoulder and nodded to Meredith. "We'll go on back now and leave you to your news gathering. Have you had a chance to interview Dawn?"

"Yes, thanks. I talked with her while the police were carrying out the raid, along with Grimes and Baxter. Quite a story. It should make all the early editions."

"Dawn? Betty's Dawn?"

Trevor was enjoying my disbelief. "The one and only. Between the two of you, this has been a night to remember. Which reminds me that Betty's still sitting in my car. If we're lucky, Dawn's gone in search of Noah's Ark with Grimes and Baxter."

CHAPTER SEVENTEEN

Invitation to the Future

Everyone agreed that Sunday dinner was the most festive affair ever. Gwen's fiancé had begun driving from Cardiff the moment he put down the phone, arriving on Meredith's doorstep before the sun peeped above the Preseli Mountains. Enid confided to me that he made up for lack of sleep by catching cat naps in the parlor while waiting for Gwen to finish shampooing and soaking in the tub. Once she emerged, sparkling clean and attired in fresh garments plucked from Enid's closet, he refused to let her out of his sight, even following her into the kitchen and joining in the food preparation.

Throughout the meal, Betty and Dawn marveled at the endless parade of Welsh culinary delights, from the first tender forkful of lamb infused with rosemary, to the wicked array of sweets stretching across the buffet. Dawn, I was pleased to observe, had dressed modestly for the occasion in a skirt and jacket of distinctive Burberry plaid. It was a fashionable – albeit expensive – outfit befitting a mother's aspirations, but no matter the cost, the purpose had been achieved: Dawn was putting forth an effort to be quiet and thoughtful. Once when

Betty caught my eye, I smiled and nodded my approval of the change that had come over her daughter.

Dawn, after all, was the heroine of the day. True, she was responsible for my failure to wear the electronic bracelet to the choir rehearsal, but she had atoned for her deed most honorably. Bit by bit, the events of the previous evening emerged, often on a wave of hearty laughter, other times with a bittersweet tinge. By the time we gathered around the dinner table, Gwen knew that her mother had died during the winter, still hoping for her daughter's return. While she could never dismiss the sorrow, the light in her eyes reflected the joy of her reunion with loved ones who never ceased caring and hoping. As I looked around the room, I pictured similar jubilation taking place in ten other homes.

If I could not grasp the unfolding of events from my own perspective, the Sunday edition of the *Western Telegraph and Cymric Times* laid it all out from start to finish, thanks to Meredith's detailed coverage. Exactly as planned, he and the police were alerted that I would be in Nevern for the choir rehearsal. They waited at headquarters, and at the first sign of movement away from that location, they dispatched men on the ground and in a helicopter to track me.

After dinner, Trevor and I sat on the sofa piecing together the events of the previous evening from our separate points of view. Safe in the crook of his arm, I listened to his account and wondered how much different the ending would have been had I remembered to wear the bracelet. Believing that I was wearing it when he dropped me at the chapel, Trevor focused on acting the thoughtful host to Betty and Dawn.

"We spent quite a bit of time wandering through Nevern," he said. "After Betty had her fill of the gift shops and historical buildings, I checked my watch and saw that rehearsal wasn't scheduled to end for another hour, so I suggested a short walk along the Pembrokeshire Path.

"It was fairly crowded because tourists and locals alike come out on Saturday evening. We watched the seals and the porpoises performing for the onlookers while several fishermen unloaded their catch, so quite a bit of time passed before Betty and I missed Dawn. Our first thought was that she might have retraced our steps, so we went back into the village. No luck. The only other explanation was that she had gone back to my car. By the time we reached the chapel, nobody was there. That's when we both started to panic. If the call from Meredith hadn't come through at that moment, I don't know what we would have done."

"What did he say?"

"That you were in a car headed north along the coast. I was on my way before he finished."

"And Betty went along with you?"

He nodded.

"Wasn't she concerned that Dawn would come back to the church and wonder what happened?"

He laughed. "That was one terrified lady until we reached the end of the line and she saw Dawn standing in the driveway. Meredith and the police were already there. They'd just discovered that we actually had been tracking Dawn who was tracking you with the help of Grimes and Baxter."

"The two who were arrested for trying to steal the Holy Cross?"

"The same. For all we know, they were planning another raid on the cave behind St. Brynach's Church. Whatever their original intention, everything changed when Dawn distracted them." His eyes twinkled. "Sound familiar?"

"Does it ever. Dawn's an expert at changing other people's plans."

"She got them on the fast track in a hurry. For a while, it appeared that they were headed directly to Aberystwyth on the main highway, but just outside of Cardigan they veered inland. Dawn said that's when it got tricky."

"Did someone mention my name?" Dawn flopped down next to Trevor.

He laughed. "Are you surprised? After all, you made the front page today."

"Nope." Dawn studied her nails intently. "I've been expecting Sarah to ask me questions like the police did."

"If you're ready to share with me, I'm dying to know the particulars," I said. "Since I haven't had time to absorb everything in the newspaper, I'd like to hear how it happened from your perspective. To go back to the beginning, why did you break away from your mother and Trevor?"

"Man, that was boring." Dawn reached for a plump Welsh tea cake on a tray atop the coffee table and took a healthy bite. "I thought we'd never stop wandering up and down the path. I saw all I wanted to see in the first five minutes and decided it wouldn't be any less fun to wait for them in the car. Nobody was paying any attention to me, so I left. I was walking up the road to the church when I saw that little guy come out of the front door. You were right behind him. Before I got near enough to call, you were following him around to the side of the building. That seemed sort of odd, so I hid behind the bushes and tried to hear what was being said. I kept watching, and when you got into the back seat of his car, I knew something funny was going on. I was sure of it when he pushed you down on the seat. The next thing I knew, he slammed the door and climbed into the driver's seat. I started yelling for help the minute he sped off with you."

"And therein lies a tale," Trevor said, giving me a nudge. "Tell Sarah what happened next, Dawn."

"Well, I was standing there screaming at the top of my lungs when a car drew up and the driver asked what was wrong. I told him I'd tell him later if he'd chase the car disappearing down the road, so he agreed and I climbed in."

"You weren't afraid to get into a car with strange men?"

"I didn't have time to be afraid. Besides, they turned out to be pretty cool. It was easy following the little guy's car while we were on the main road, but once he turned onto a side road, it was a lot harder keeping pace. Pretty soon, a helicopter showed up. The guys figured we were near a military base and it was about to land, but no matter which way we turned, it stayed right with us. It made so much noise I had trouble hearing what they were saying.

"The further we went, the narrower the road became until it was only a single lane. The driver — I think his name is Ray — is chubby and looks like a nerd, but he knows his way around a race track. Whenever another car got in our way, Ray honked like a demon and forced it off to the side so we could pass.

"The road was really twisty and every time the car ahead slowed for to a curve, the brakes went on. That's how we kept them in sight most of the time. When we came to one crossroad, Ray wasn't sure which way to go, but Ken, the other guy, pointed to the right and said something about Florida."

"The ruins of Strata Florida Abbey," Trevor said. "It's where the monks of Glastonbury first brought what some people believe is the Holy Grail."

"Whatever," Dawn said. "Anyway, we went in the other direction, and it's a good thing, because pretty soon we saw the tail lights of the car up ahead. It was slowing down to turn into a long driveway. We couldn't see anything behind the hedge except the chimneys of a large house. Ray wasn't sure what we should do. He thought it might be some kind of a hideout for gangsters and was afraid we'd be trapped, so we parked at the side of the road. Before we figured out what to do next, the helicopter landed in the road ahead of us and a policeman got out with his gun drawn."

"You must have been scared."

Dawn nodded. "I was, like, totally spooked. I thought I'd been riding with a couple of criminals when the policeman told Ray and Ken to step out of the car with their hands up. He was frisking them when another policeman pulled up. The minute he came over to the car and looked at me, he started yelling to the others that I wasn't Sarah Morgan. He grabbed my arm and asked how I got the bracelet, so I told him I tried it on and decided to wear it, but that wasn't important because Sarah had been kidnapped and we were trying to save her."

"That was Sergeant Floyd," Trevor said. "He sent word to Meredith, who was in a car not far behind the police, and Meredith relayed the information to me. At that point, I was probably two miles behind him. I didn't reach the estate until it was surrounded."

"Estate?"

"This is where the synchronicity comes in, Sarah. Remember Meredith telling about the old lady who thinks she owns what's left of the Holy Grail?"

"Yes. Well, go on."

"Her estate is Nanteos. It's connected by tunnels with Strata Florida. The tunnels and underground rooms have been unused for hundreds of years. Leave it to Phil to con her into believing that they're occupied by ghosts, spirits, and whatever you want to call them of the past. She's well along in years, more than a little dotty by now and easy prey for Phil."

"Exactly what did he do?"

"He convinced her that the forest nymphs inhabiting the premises asked him to help them reveal the key to eternal life at the Eisteddfod. At her age, that sounded like a worthy reason for allowing him and his wife to move in and appropriate her valuable harpsichord for nymph rehearsals."

I tried not to laugh. "It's all so absurd. And yet it

could have ended in tragedy. It's a miracle that the women Phil kidnapped retained their sanity locked away from family and friends."

Trevor nodded toward Gwen sitting in the corner with her fiancé, their arms wrapped around each other, their whispered conversation interrupted by frequent kisses. "If Gwen's any example, they'll all make up for lost time. It takes youth and strength of character to live through an ordeal like that. Even though Phil claims he meant them no harm, what he and his wife did was so bizarre that no excuse can rectify the matter. Each young woman lost a piece of her life, anything from a month to a year. That time is gone forever."

"Do you suppose anyone connected with the Eisteddfod knew Phil's plans?"

"I'm sure that none of them put it all together. The director told Meredith that Phil entered three groups for the program: his male choir, the women's choir, and a select choir. The names of the members don't have to be listed, just the number of singers so the officials know how many risers are needed. In his registration, he indicated that the select choir had twelve members. Enough said."

"Obviously Phil and Laura will be put on trial, but what will happen to the old lady?"

At that moment, Trevor's Mum came by to replace the empty tray of Welsh cakes on the coffee table with a batch fresh from the oven.

"Oh, yummy," Dawn said. She selected several before excusing herself.

Mrs. Evans watched her go, a half-smile on her face. "An interesting young lady. Betty has been helping

Enid and me in the kitchen. From what she tells us, Dawn is something of a handful, but nothing that a few years won't help. Apparently Betty lost her husband several years ago. Raising children is a chore without a man to enforce rules. It must be even harder today than it was for me while you and Meredith were going through the teen years. In any event, we have to give Dawn credit for the way she rose to the occasion yesterday."

"That she did," Trevor said. "Credit goes to a lot of people who helped pull off the rescue, including the would-be treasure hunters."

Mrs. Evans signed. "There are happy endings for everyone except that poor old lady. The elderly cling to their homes as long as possible, but it's clear that she needs a caretaker, far more than someone once a week to clean. Meredith tells me she'll be admitted to the home for the elderly in Newcastle Emlyn if a full-time companion isn't found immediately."

"That's probably the best solution," Trevor said. "In her state, she was no match for Phil and his wife. Apparently they convinced her that nymphs inhabiting her property would give her the gift of eternal life."

Mrs. Evans clucked her tongue. "Sad to say, she's living in a make-believe world. Sometimes I think that we Welsh love our legends too much."

Trevor nodded in accord. "You may be right, Mum. No reflection on the way you brought us up, but it starts in early childhood. Parents and teachers drum Welsh history into our brains, but our heroes aren't kings and queens. They're holy men and women and wizards. Most were real people, but oral tradition credits them with mythic deeds."

Mrs. Evans nodded. "They become very real to Welsh children, not like Cinderella and Sleeping Beauty whose storybook castles exist only in the mind. Here in Wales we can reach out and touch the magical places, the mountain caves where mystics lived and ancient chapels where miracles occurred."

I sat up. "And St. Non's holy well?"

Trevor tossed me a grin. "Exactly." He reached out and caught his mother's sleeve. "Mum, Sarah and I visited the well, just like you and my father did before you were married."

She flushed with delight. Her voice dropped to a whisper. "I hope you two made a wish."

In unison, we answered in the affirmative.

"Then you will be truly blessed. Now Sarah, please don't peg me as a dotty Welsh woman. Maybe the power of the well water exists, and maybe it's nothing more than a legend. All I know is that I had an ideal marriage and two wonderful sons. I can wish you and Trevor no better than that."

She bent down and kissed me on the forehead. "And now if you'll excuse me, I smell a fresh batch of cakes in the oven waiting to be rescued."

"Another Welsh legend has legs, and I'm certainly not one to dispute the matter," Trevor said. He was just about to kiss me when a muffled sound interrupted his train of thought. "See what you do to me, Sarah? I'm hearing bells."

I pushed him away playfully. "You overestimate me. We're hearing my cell phone. It must have fallen out of my pocket." The very next ring pinpointed its exact location, wedged deeply between sofa cushions. "It's bound to be Elspeth."

He grinned. "Just so it's not another suitor."

After my initial "Hello," Elspeth gushed forth non-stop.

"Sarah, Tara, what a coup! I couldn't believe my ears when I turned on the BBC Newscast. How are you feeling? Were you really kidnapped? Did you have any idea that you would find the missing ladies alive? You've solved the mystery of the year. How soon do you think you can finish the book? I'm writing up a contract as we speak. I'll be around to your flat first thing tomorrow morning so you can sign it before you leave for Hatchard's. Now the next thing we need to do is..."

"Whoa, Elspeth. I can't process everything you're saying. So much has happened in such a short amount of time."

"Three weeks on your tour and you're a celebrity already with everyone dying to read your next book."

"They'll have a bit of a wait. I haven't started writing it."

"I know, I know, but it won't take you long. We have a best seller on our hands without a word set on paper."

"You're an optimist, Elspeth. Still, I have to admit it's a good story."

"Good? It would be the story of the hour if it weren't for your other story."

I hesitated. "You're talking about *The Rittenhouse Murder*?"

"No, silly. I'm talking about the headlines in all

the tabloids."

"What headlines? What tabloids?"

I heard the shuffling of newspapers as Elspeth lined up her evidence. "Listen to this: 'Tara tantalizes *Torquaytoon's* Trevor.' Here's another: 'Kidnapped author is kissy-kissy with Evans.' And this one reads: '*Toon* hunk falls for fab femme.' The secret's out, Sarah. You've been uncovered as a twosome. Think of all those broken hearts."

"You're making me blush, Elspeth. How did that get out?"

"The British press is notoriously nosy and last night's rescue helped them put it all together. The newscasters identified all the people who showed up at the site, not just the women involved. Trevor's presence added a whole fascinating dimension. And when some of the reporters remembered seeing you both on the Sophia Plus Six show, the fans made the connection in a hurry. The telly ran clips of you two dancing together on the show. You both had romantic gleams in your eyes early on."

Throughout my conversation with Elspeth, Trevor had been nuzzling my neck, unaware that he was the topic of conversations throughout Great Britain. Smiling, not saying a word, I passed the phone to him.

He grinned back at me. "Why are you looking at me that way? Anything wrong?"

"I'll let you decide, Toon hunk. Here. You'd better speak with Elspeth. She can fill you in on the latest news."

Scarcely ten seconds into their conversation, he got the picture. After enjoying a hearty laugh, he said,

"That's what I get for falling in love with a wacko on the train and living in a fishbowl. I'm beginning to think that I'm turning into one of my characters."

I challenged him with a mock-belligerent scowl. "A wacko?"

He drew me close. "A fabulous wacko who stole my heart the minute she attacked me. A spectacular wacko who I'm marrying next weekend, if she's willing to fit it into her book tour."

I gazed up at the subject of my dearest wish. "I'm more than willing, even if you do think I'm a wacko."

"Then that's settled." He kissed me soundly before resuming his phone conversation. "Did you hear that, Elspeth? After next week, Sarah's tour will take a back seat to romance. We prefer to honeymoon in private. I trust you're agreeable."

It was difficult to decipher Elspeth's exact reply words, but the excited whoops barreling through the ether confirmed her unrestricted approval.

"I'm glad you're on our side, Elspeth," he said. "Just one request: not a word to anyone until the deed is done....Thanks. We appreciate your willingness to uphold that confidence...Sarah will notify you when the details are arranged...As of now, we expect it to be a very simple and quiet service with only the family and some elusive Welsh spirits in attendance."

As he rang off, an apologetic expression crossed his face. "I didn't mean to overstep my bounds, Sarah. The wedding plans should be up to the bride. I was caught up in the moment, thinking how beautiful it would be to be married with the cliffs and the ocean as a backdrop."

"On the Pembrokeshire Path near St. Non's well?"

He nodded.

"Two minds with a single thought," I said, raising my lips to his.

Once every sweet was consumed and the Sunday dinner dishes were cleared away, we joined Meredith and the twins in the garden, my last opportunity to absorb the serenity of the Pembrokeshire coast before fulfilling the remaining commitments on my hectic book tour. Earlier, Trevor and I agreed that the late afternoon express to London was the best option for the four of us, Betty and Dawn included. With but three days remaining before their return flight to the States, Betty wanted to cover some important sites they had missed, like Hampton Court, the Tower of London, and the London Museum. So it was that our animated conversation and reluctant goodbyes mingled with the twins' hearty laughter, drowning out the sound of knocking at the front door. Undeterred, the caller was persistent, and presently our chatter was interrupted by halloos.

Betty was the first to spot the two men rounding the side of the cottage. "Oh, it's Ray and Ken. I've been hoping you'd find us."

Trevor and I glanced at each other, stunned. "The treasure-hunters?" I mouthed.

The corners of his eyes crinkled with mirth. "None other. Astounding. And on a first name basis, at that."

Betty marched over to Ray and took him by the arm. "Everybody, I'd like you to meet these two wonderful men. Even if you weren't there last evening, you know by now that they helped my daughter chase the driver who was kidnapping Sarah. Because of their bravery, Gwen and all the other girls held captive are home with their loved ones. What a glorious day!"

While Betty introduced the two men to Mrs. Evans, Enid, Gwen, and her fiancé, Meredith sidled over to us, an incredulous expression on his face. "One has to wonder what those blokes are up to. Knowing their reputations, Betty could be the open sesame to a new adventure."

He did not have long to wait for an explanation. Betty, the two men in tow, hurried to my side. "This has been such an incredible weekend. I wouldn't have missed it for the world and I hate to run off from you and Trevor, but Ray has offered to drive Dawn and me back to London. He says he can get us tickets to a Globe Theatre performance on Tuesday. He thinks it will be a perfect ending to Dawn's first trip to England."

"One of the actors is a former student of mine," Ray said. "Dawn will enjoy meeting him."

Trevor and I exchanged glances. The laughter in his eyes told me that he already was developing a Dawn-like character for "Torquaytoons."

"And best of all, Ray and Ken are planning to visit us in the States very soon," Betty added. "They've even invited us to help them investigate an early site in Kentucky."

Meredith stopped in his tracks. "Did I hear someone mention an early site? What kind of a site?"

"A Welsh site," Ken rubbed his hands together in

anticipation. "I've discovered documents that prove there were two King Arthurs."

Meredith rolled his eyes. Ken, oblivious, continued with unabated enthusiasm. We've all read about King Arthur Number One since childhood, but not many know about King Arthur II."

"Count me among the ignorant," Meredith said, under his breath.

Ken chattered on, happy in his own little world. "He was part of a trans-Atlantic migration from Wales in the 6th century. They made deep inroads into the wilderness until they reached what is now Kentucky. Indians killed him there and his companions embalmed him. Afterward, they brought him back to Wales and buried him at Mynydd-y-Gaer, near Bridgend."

Meredith, the consummate reporter had whipped out his notebook and was jotting notes as fast as Ken spoke. "Any idea how they got the wherewithal to embalm him?"

Ken stopped midway in his speech. "I haven't gone into that yet, but perhaps we'll uncover that information once we arrive there."

Meredith pressed on. "What proof do you have that King Arthur II existed?"

Ken clasped his hands together and gazed skyward, as if receiving a communication from outer space. "The inscriptions, of course. They left tablets written in Coelbren, an ancient British alphabet, saying that the Welsh migrated there after a huge comet devastated large areas of Britain."

Trevor grinned. "So the Welsh arrived in America before Columbus?"

"My goodness, yes," Ken said. "It was discovered by the Welsh prince Madoc and his followers. Ray and I expect to find more tablets written in Coelbren as we work our way through Kentucky. This will open an exciting new chapter of history."

By the time Betty and Dawn had returned to the guest cottage to pack their bags and were ready to depart with Grimes and Baxter, Meredith had done some sleuthing. He nudged Trevor. "I called John Wilson. When he stopped laughing, he told me that CADW historians dismiss Coelbren as a 19th century hoax. Shall I tell Betty that she's about to drive off into the sunset with a couple of charlatans?"

Trevor poked me. "Do you feel another plot coming on?"

I returned his grin. "One at a time, please."

We walked Betty and Dawn to Ray's car. As they were getting settled in the back seat, Meredith stuck his head through the window. "By the way, Baxter, what's playing at the Globe on Tuesday?"

Ray switched on the ignition. "Seems to me it's 'All's Well That Ends Well.'"

Trevor laughed aloud. "My sentiments exactly." The car bearing the unlikely quartet had pulled away when he added, "Everyone deserves a happy ending. If I read them properly, those rogues are romantics at heart."

"Like the murderous man on the train who turned out to be my true love?"

"Exactly like him." Pulling me close, he kissed me so thoroughly that we never heard Meredith and Enid retrace their steps to the backyard where their lively twins were clamoring for another of Trevor's imaginary journeys. There would be ample time for their flights of fancy in days to come. Now it was our turn.

Made in the USA
Lexington, KY
16 July 2012